Last Night at the Jolly Chicken

Misplaced Adventures

Last Night at the Jolly Chicken

EDITED BY KEVIN PETTWAY

Cursed Dragon Ship
PUBLISHING

Copyright © 2023 by Misplaced Adventures

Don't Touch the Damned Card Copyright © 2023 by Todd Fahnestock

Short Straws Reprint Copyright © 2023 by Kevin J. Anderson

Wandering Monsters Reprint Copyright © 2023 by Jody Lynn Nye

Cursed Dragon Ship Publishing, LLC

6046 FM 2920 Rd, #231, Spring, TX 77379

captwyvern@curseddragonship.com

Cover © 2023 by Lena Shore

Art © 2022 by Bad Carrot Studios

Proofread by S.G. George

ISBN 978-1-951445-45-4

ISBN 978-1-951445-46-1 (ebook)

All rights reserved

No part of this book may be reproduced in any form or by any electronic or mechanical means, including information storage and retrieval systems, without written permission from the publisher, except for the use of brief quotations in a book review.

This book is a work of fiction fresh from the author's imagination. Any resemblance to actual persons or places is mere coincidence.

CONTENTS

Misplaced Adventures Novels	vii
Introduction	xi
Don't Touch the Damned Card *Todd Fahnestock*	1
Meanwhile in the Jolly Chicken *Part One*	18
The Blossom Queen *C.M. McGuire*	23
Meanwhile in the Jolly Chicken *Part Two*	43
Local Cuisine *Ethan A. Cooper*	44
Meanwhile in the Jolly Chicken *Part Three*	72
Gizella of the Vulg *William LJ Galaini*	73
Meanwhile in the Jolly Chicken *Part Four*	94
Wandering Monsters *Jody Lynn Nye*	95
Meanwhile in the Jolly Chicken *Part Five*	109
Between a Rock and a Hard Place *Jessica Raney*	110
Meanwhile in the Jolly Chicken *Part Six*	125
Nobody's That Stupid *Jen Bair*	127
Meanwhile in the Jolly Chicken *Part Seven*	151
Short Straws *Kevin J. Anderson*	153
Meanwhile in the Jolly Chicken *Part Eight*	165
The Wrong Way to Build a Sex Dungeon *Kevin Pettway*	166
Meanwhile in the Jolly Chicken *Part Nine*	192

Acknowledgments	193
Author Bios	195
Join the Cursed Dragon Ship Newsletter	201

MISPLACED ADVENTURES NOVELS

Anthology
Last Night at the Jolly Chicken

<u>Misplaced Mercenaries</u> by Kevin Pettway
A Good Running Away
Blow Out the Candle When You Leave
Big Damn Magic
Illusions of Decency
Heroes Kill Everyone

<u>Hettie Stormheart</u> by Jen Bair
One Good Eye

For our publisher, Kelly, for believing in us, working like hell for us, and accepting all the blame for us.

INTRODUCTION

I first met Kevin Pettway at a writers convention where we happened to sit next to each. At one of the evening events, authors were encouraged to read the first page of their current project. Kevin read the beginning of his fourth book in the *Misplaced Mercenaries* series and I was instantly intrigued. (I subsequently made him take that particular novel out of the sequence because it didn't fit. Though he'll claim it was because I'm mean. A little of both might be true.)

Luckily, I convinced him to send me a sample of the first book in that series, *A Good Running Away,* and I fell in love. The novel is full of outrageous adventure with heart-wrenching emotional scenes all sprinkled with humor and creative swearing. I was so in love, I offered Kevin a publishing contract to be the first author in brand spanking new Cursed Dragon Ship Publishing. What happened later will take up much more room than I have available in this short intro. Suffuse it to say, that *Misplaced Mercenaries* garnered a loyal following among us and readers of sword and sorcery at large.

So much so that when the series came to an end, no one wanted the fun to stop. Since I couldn't chain Kevin to his desk to do nothing but write, we enlisted the talent of five fantasy writers to join the ranks. Jen Bair, Jessica Raney, William LJ Galaini, C.M. McGuire, and Ethan A. Cooper went through rigorous interviews and tests to qualify to join Kevin Pettway. (Actually, we just read their other works and made sure they had a sense of humor. If you've never had to sit through a series of dad jokes for a job interview, what have you been doing your whole life?)

In the end, we created the *Misplaced Adventures* to expand Kevin's original creation and keep the shenanigans coming. Each author has taken hold of a different part of the continent and created an entire series from that point. One book from a different author will release every two months from this point until it stops being fun. To kick off the adventure, this anthology introduces the reader to characters from the minds of each of these creative minds as well as three guest authors who agreed to join in on the mischief. Kevin wrote the italicized tidbits that tie each story together.

We hope you get as much joy out of reading the *Misplaced Adventures* as we have creating them.

Kelly Lynn Colby
Editorial Director
Cursed Dragon Ship Publishing

DON'T TOUCH THE DAMNED CARD
TODD FAHNESTOCK

Slayter the Mage

Slayter was bored.

One wouldn't think attempting to save the world would be boring, what with digging into a mystery that stretched back two thousand years where the fate of the entire world hung in the balance, hung on every detail Slayter could unearth.

But apparently one would be wrong.

Slayter was so close to truly important answers that he could almost touch them. Almost! He just wanted to reach out his fingers and—

But no. Between home and the answers lay fields and dirt roads. And more fields and more dirt roads. Worse, he'd seen these fields before. He'd traveled these dirt roads before. Even the sky was old and tired looking, a languid blue devoid of clouds. Anything would be better. Perhaps a rogue band of brigands suddenly riding toward them, swords waving. Or a hungry Kyolar escaped from the noktum, teeth gnashing.

Even Slayter's horse seemed dulled by the monotony, clopping forward slowly as if the tall grass fields would go on and on and on. All Slayter had were fields, this lethargic horse, and ...

And Khyven.

Slayter turned his gaze over to the tall warrior who rode next to him on the violent monster he called a horse. Khyven glared ahead at the road like it had offended him. He'd been glaring exactly that way for hours. He was probably bored too. Maybe getting angry was how Khyven fought off the boredom. It *was* his fallback answer to anything that didn't go his way. Step one: hate it. Step two: kill it.

Khyven was exceedingly useful to have around if there was violence. He could kill better than any single person Slayter had ever met.

If only there were some brigands.

Slayter fell to studying the details of the tall warrior, details he'd studied extensively before, but which were newly more interesting than the unending fields he'd studied for the last four hours.

The warrior wore an armory of small and large blades, most notably his three swords: two at his left hip and one in a sheath across his back.

The first was a normal steel sword, a serviceable blade that could hack a man to pieces quite neatly in Khyven's capable hands.

The second was a deliciously alluring Mavric iron sword. Only Giants made weapons out of Mavric iron, and only Giants could wield them. If a normal Human tried, their flesh would begin to bubble after a day or so. By day two or three, their muscles and skin would slough off their bones and they'd die in horrible agony. Khyven was the exception. He could not only carry the sword, he could wreak havoc with it.

The third sword was an arena practice sword carved out of solid hardwood, a gift from their mutual friend, Vohn. It had the words *The Diplomat* burned into one side. That was a story.

Vohn had rebuked Khyven numerous times, said he couldn't just go around killing people when they displeased him. He had to be diplomatic. The next day Khyven had rescued Shalure from a shkazat den, and he'd killed no one to do it. Instead, the bouncer, the barkeep, and five other patrons—all of whom had tried to manhandle Khyven—had come away with broken bones and bloody noses. Vohn had made him the sword as a joke. Khyven carried it as a solution, beating the snot out of his foes with a glorified club and calling it diplomacy.

There. Khyven had been studied again. How long had that taken?

Slayter glanced at the sky, hoping the sun would be low on the horizon, that his scrutiny had taken at least two hours, but the thing had barely moved.

A blue glow off to his right caught Slayter's attention. He sat up straight in his saddle. The glow nestled in the long grass, lighting them, making them look like little spears of enchanted steel.

Well, *that* wasn't boring at all, not anywhere in the vicinity of boring.

That was magic.

Slayter pulled his mount to a stop. Khyven slowed instinctively as though he was connected to Slayter's body by strings. The warrior was always on alert. Ever since he overthrew the usurper of Usara and swore fealty to the queen, he'd been angrily protective of her inner circle, which included Slayter. He'd saved all their lives a number of times.

Khyven's basket of weapons and his superlative fighting skills were also married to heightened perceptions and a keen sense of his surroundings. He had reflexes that would shame a mountain lion and the eyesight of a hawk.

And yet he hadn't noticed the blue glow.

"Do you see that?" Slayter pointed.

"See what?" Khyven's eyes narrowed as he scanned the field, his gaze passing right over the area without seeing it.

"You don't see the blue glow."

"Slayter, you're doing it again. You have to actually tell me what you're talking about. I can't just—"

"Well, that is just *fascinating*." Slayter guided his mount off the road and into the field.

"Wait!" Khyven yanked his reins, but his horse—a mean-spirited stallion Khyven had named Hellface—tossed his head and almost shrugged Khyven off his back. Contrary to Khyven's ridiculous talent at everything physical, he was a lousy horseman. So, of course, he had chosen a nearly impossible horse as his mount in some odd bid to prove he wasn't terrible at it.

Slayter didn't understand that logic, but then most people's motivations defied understanding. He moved closer to the strange blue glow.

"Slayter, if you would just—" Hellface spun in a circle, jerked to a stop, and spun in the other direction; dislodging Khyven. He tumbled to the ground awkwardly, disentangling himself from the stirrups. Somehow he landed on his feet, spinning to a crouch with stunning grace. The stallion leaned in to take a bite out of Khyven's shoulder.

Khyven cursed and elbowed the horse out of the way, just enough to make it miss. Hellface shook his head with a snort and backed up, looking for another opportunity.

Slayter drew nearer the blue glow, pulled his horse to a stop, and painstakingly dismounted; maneuvering his metal prosthetic leg out of the stirrup and gingerly putting it on the ground. It really was a marvel of engineering, but Slayter still couldn't balance properly on it. He almost fell over as he awkwardly yanked his good leg out of the stirrup. After wobbling and stumbling, he righted himself and turned to face his prize.

It was a glowing blue card, slightly larger than a playing card, laying there in the grass for no apparent reason.

"Would you just wait?" Khyven dodged another bite from Hellface, leaped off the road, and ran through the waist-high grass. He was, of course, ridiculously fast. Slayter had seen the man cross dozens of feet like he'd teleported. He arrived at Slayter's side in a second. Hellface stayed on the road. The big black horse simply stood there watching Khyven with narrowed eyes as though plotting his revenge. The strange thing about Hellface was he'd had several opportunities to run off during this journey, and he never did. For a creature that seemed to hate its rider, it didn't have any interest in escaping.

"It's a card," Slayter said.

Slayter was a Line Mage, which meant he could access a little bit of each of the other four types of magic—Love Magic, Lore Magic, Life Magic, and Land Magic—if he inscribed the correct spell upon a surface and channeled his lifeforce through it. He kept a cylinder of clay disks—each holding a nearly prepared spell—at his side, and he withdrew one of the disks now. With a metal scratcher, he completed the final line, activating the spell. Orange light flared from the symbol. The light should have also flared around the card, showing that it was magical.

It didn't. Instead, a halo of orange light flared around Slayter's head. Slayter snapped the disk, dissipating the spell and ceasing its drain on him.

"Oh, that is fascinating," he said.

"What is it?" Khyven asked.

"The spell is cast on me. It's literally a figment of my imagination. The card isn't really there."

"What card?"

"I see a card." Slayter knelt in the grass next to the thing.

"Well don't touch it!" Khyven warned.

"I can't actually touch it. It's an illusion. The question is, why put it here? If it is focused on me, how did it know I was going to be here? There really is so much to know." He thought for a moment. "I'm going to have to touch it."

"I said *don't* touch it!"

"The spell is already working upon me, clearly. Touching it will likely complete whatever is meant to happen."

"*Meant* to ... What if it's meant to *kill* you?"

"Not everything is about killing, Khyven."

"I didn't mean ... I wasn't ... I don't just go around killing people!" he said for what must have been the twentieth time in the last few months.

"It is far more likely someone is trying to get my attention. It could be important."

"Or it could be a trap."

"It could be just about anything. We could sit here and speculate forever."

"Or we could get back on our horses and continue on our mission."

"The only way to know for sure is to try." Slayter withdrew a second spell, completed all but the barest scratch with his metal pen, then he poised his fingernail over it.

"No." Khyven shook his head.

Slayter reached out and touched the glowing card.

"Slayter—"

The field vanished. The sky and the sun vanished.

Slayter and Khyven now stood in the middle of a tavern. Wooden rafters hung low overhead. Rough wooden benches and tables lined the far wall, and an oak bar stood on the other side.

The tavern was packed with travelers. Most of them looked like they were prepared to wade into a war. One had full plate mail armor with flanges rising from the shoulder plates so tall that the man certainly couldn't see to his left or right. Not that his full helmet would have allowed that anyway. He—or she, really, it was impossible to tell—sat at a table with three others, similarly armored.

At the next table sat what looked like a human with a white and purple unicorn head. Or was that an elaborate helm? To its left and right sat what looked like two greasy thieves from Usara's wharf.

A third table held what Slayter guessed was a mage. The young man wore a green robe, a green conical cap, and spectacles like Vohn. Sitting in the chair next to him was a giant badger?

Yes, it couldn't be anything other than a badger, Slayter decided.

There had to be a dozen and a half tables in the tavern, each similarly filled, all save one. Slayter wondered if that table was reserved for Khyven and himself. The pair of them might actually fit in this motley gathering in a strange kind of way, like a scrap of paper fit into a collection of odds and ends that were anything but paper.

"Now aren't you glad I touched the card?" Slayter asked. This was marvelously curious.

"Am I glad? No." Khyven's gaze darted from one group to another, no doubt assessing each as a potential threat. He didn't draw his sword, which told Slayter that Khyven didn't see anything immediately dangerous. He never drew unless the fight was on. One of the secrets to his fighting success was that Khyven was actually magical himself. He had an odd form of Land or Lore Magic—frustratingly, Slayter didn't know which—that allowed him to "see" threats come at him in the form of a blue wind. If one of these fearsome fighters decided to attack, Khyven would know it before the strike ever landed. "Where are we?"

"Well, I imagine we are going to find that out shortly."

"Because?"

"Because we were brought here."

At that moment, as if on cue, a slither of magic pushed into Slayter's mind. It took hold of his thoughts and made the idea of dropping his arms to his sides and relaxing a particularly pleasing idea. Slayter now very much wanted to do it, and he retained only enough of his self-possession to resist long enough to do what he had planned to do before he touched the card.

He scraped the last line in the clay disk with his fingernail.

Magic rushed through him. The disk flared with orange light.

The compulsion that had nearly dominated his mind fled before the fire of his magic. It was like the tendrils of mind control were rivulets of water spreading throughout his brain, and the counterspell was the heat of a blacksmith's forge. The tendrils hissed and evaporated, and Slayter regained command of his mind.

He extended the spell to encompass Khyven, who had begun to rise from his combat crouch into a docile, sheep-like stance. When the spell burned through Khyven's mind, he snarled. His steel sword flashed out of its sheath.

"Wait!" Slayter held up his hand.

"Slayter, someone just tried to control my mind."

"I know. Isn't it curious?"

"No, it's—curious?" Khyven shot him an incredulous look. "There's a room full of armed people. And that," he pointed at the green-robed mage, who was now on alert and looking at Khyven with narrowed eyes, "is probably a mage."

Khyven's off-hand suddenly held a dagger. He'd drawn it so fast Slayter hadn't even seen it.

"Put away the steel," Slayter said. "Please."

Khyven showed his teeth. In a flash the blade vanished, and the Diplomat appeared in his hand.

Really. How did he do that so fast?

Activating the mind-control counterspell had pulled a good amount of energy from Slayter. The mind-control spell was strong, and the longer Slayter held his counterspell, the weaker he would become. Best find the source quickly.

He turned and scanned the room. An enormous troll stood in the back, towering over the rest of the clientele. He was big enough for the steel-tipped horns atop his head to almost reach the low rafters.

The troll's piggy eyes fixed on Khyven. Its craggy face was set into a stony look of nothing. Practically nothing. Perhaps slightly annoyed. The troll could have been just another odd traveler in this place, but there were two reasons Slayter didn't think so.

First, the rest of the adventurers in the tavern looked like they were waiting for ... something. Their turn, maybe. The troll looked like a bouncer. A big, ugly axe dangled from his gnarled fingers, and two more were strapped to his back.

Second, the troll seemed to be standing in an innocuous corner of the room. It was empty, draped in shadow, yet the creature seemed like he was protecting something.

That piqued Slayter's curiosity. He studied the troll's immediate surroundings. There were no chairs or tables behind him, not even a door that might lead to a closet or another room. There weren't even any wall hangings—

Oh wait. Yes, there was, but it was so small on the big, shadowy wall that Slayter had missed it at first glance. It was a card, an illustrated card stuck to the wall.

Slayter itched to cast another detect magic spell, but he held back. That card *had* to be what the troll was protecting. It was suspiciously the same size as the glowing blue card in the field, the teleportation trigger that had brought them here.

"It's the card," Slayter said to Khyven.

"What?" Khyven growled.

Slayter sighed. He did his best to speak as clearly and concisely as possible, but Khyven simply wasn't as quick to figure things out as he was to kill them.

Then the card spoke. It actually spoke. The thing was alive!

"They're not under my control," it said.

Slayter felt a familiar odd feeling, like great magic was being cast nearby. Sometimes when someone used magic, he could feel it even if he hadn't created a detect magic spell. It was like two giant hands invisible hands pressed on his back and chest at the same time. He felt that now.

Then the room broke into pandemonium.

Khyven the Unkillable

"It's the card," Slayter said, as though that was supposed to mean something.

Khyven growled. "What?"

Slayter was a walking cipher. He flung mysterious phrases into the air all the time, but no one could ever understand them until it was too late. The mage was a genius. His mind worked down several roads at one time and several steps ahead of anyone else, even Queen Rhenn's inner circle, which was made up of the smartest people Khyven had ever met. But Slayter's big brain rarely helped Khyven until after the violence was done.

The troll launched himself at Khyven.

What Slayter called Khyven's "magic" activated. Until meeting Queen Rhenn's inner circle, Khyven had always thought the blue wind was just a heightening of his awareness, a product of the fighting skills he'd honed over a hundred battles. Now he knew different. It was magic, and it could actually predict the future.

A powerful gust of translucent blue wind shot at Khyven. It was shaped like a wide-bladed axe, preceding the troll's attack. Khyven spun to the side and the blue wind sliced by him. That ugly axe slammed down to Khyven's left, splintering floorboards.

The creature had fully expected to split Khyven in half. The troll's attack had been frighteningly fast, and if not for the blue wind, he would have succeeded.

But he had missed, and suddenly being without a target left him overextended. Khyven leapt onto the troll's stooped back, planted both feet, and delivered three quick strikes with the Diplomat: left ear, right ear, and right temple, mind the horns.

He launched off and shoved the creature hard as he did a backflip and landed on the floor.

The troll stumbled past, crashing into tables full of the other warriors and thieves in the room. The thing was tough. Those strikes would have broken a human's skull, but the troll seemed only dazed and tried sluggishly to get up. The two who'd been crushed underneath the troll weren't getting up at all.

Khyven spun to Slayter. "What *about* the card? I don't know what—"

Everyone in the tavern stood up. Chairs scraped back, some toppled over and clattered to the floor. Swords rang on scabbards. Daggers slid from sheaths. The lone wizard in the green robes leveled his staff at Khyven.

"Slayter, what did you do?" Khyven roared.

"Keep them busy," Slayter said.

"Keep them *busy*?"

The entire room charged Khyven while Slayter marched up to the far wall upon which hung a small card.

It's the card. The mage's words returned to him.

Okay, so *that* was the card, but what did it have to do with anything?

Spears of blue wind came at Khyven from all directions. The most important, though, was a tornado wind that came from the green-robed mage with the staff. The staff's green gem glowed like it was about to explode.

Khyven flung his dagger underhanded and dropped to the ground. The blade hit the staff, knocking it upward just a hair. Green fire blasted just above where Khyven had been, cutting a path through the room and blowing an eight-foot circle in the roof above the far wall. A tall man charging Khyven from behind screamed and tried to pat out his burning hair.

All right. So these people weren't going to worry about hurting each other. They wouldn't hesitate to attack him even if one of the others was in the way.

Khyven rolled to the side as a sword plunged into the wooden floor behind him. He kicked out another fighter's knee as a dagger spun past his head. He rolled to his feet in time to dodge a longbow that whipped past his shoulder. The woman wielding it held onto it like a two-handed club, but she missed, hitting the chair next to him instead. He punched her in the stomach.

She flew backward and crashed into two other fighters. All three went down in a tangle of chair legs and people legs.

Because of the fallen troll, the archer tangle, and the green mage's blast, there was a breathless moment where no whispers of blue wind came at Khyven. He took the half-second to glance at Slayter.

The mage stood before the card perched on the wall, talking to it.

"A story? You brought us here for a *story*?"

"It's time to go!" Khyven shouted.

"A moment." Slayter held up a dismissive hand like Khyven was a child trying to pull his mother away from the dress rack at a bazaar.

"Slayter, I'm—" But that was the end of Khyven's reprieve. Spears of blue wind came at him from all around. A short, burly bruiser leaped at him, swinging a mace at his knees. A tall, lanky man in a loose, open peasant shirt sauntered toward him.

The green mage had regrouped and pointed his staff at Khyven again. Another tornado of blue wind whooshed out. Khyven jumped over the mace, dove low to avoid the lanky man's rapier strike, picked up the archer's fallen bow, and flung it at the mage's head.

The bow smashed into the bridge of the mage's nose. Blood spattered and the mage fell backward. His staff blew a hole in the ceiling directly over his head this time. Heavy rafters and bits of stone dropped on him. He crumpled to the floor and didn't get up again.

Khyven grunted, muscles flexing as he reversed his momentum in an instant. He sidestepped toward the surprised bruiser, who had almost brought his mace back up. Khyven kicked him in the head. The short man went down, skidding across the floor like an upended turtle.

The lanky man saluted with his rapier, a lopsided smile on his face, and he moved in, well-balanced, catlike. A duelist.

Khyven smiled. It was true he often couldn't understand Slayter, but he did understand this. This was the fight, and the fight was where he lived. The man wanted a duel, and Khyven was happy to oblige.

The blue wind lashed out, quick as a snake's tongue. Khyven leaned to the side, dodging the blade, sheathing the Diplomat, and drawing his steel sword in the same motion. He spun and brought his sword up in time to block the second strike, aimed for his neck. The duelist was fast!

It was impossible for Khyven to unsee the blue wind, but he did his best to ignore it. It was, after all, a form of cheating. This was a good fight was between equals. He wanted to test this man's mettle for real.

The duelist's blade flicked out once, twice, three times, lightning fast: a hack to the right, to the left, then a straightforward thrust. Khyven caught the first strike on his sword, the second on his parrying dagger, then he executed a stop-thrust. It was a difficult maneuver to pull with a longsword, especially against a rapier, but if one was strong enough and fast enough, one could do it. And most opponents, especially rapier fighters, didn't expect you to do that. It could lend the element of surprise.

Lanky's eyes went wide as Khyven batted his rapier aside.

Suddenly the duelist had a longsword sticking out of his fighting shoulder. With a whimper, he fell back.

A pile of broken chairs, overturned tables, and limp bodies had grown around Khyven, but still the tavern patrons came on. A wiry man spinning a bolo clambered over an upended table like a spider. A flash of blue wind spun at Khyven. He pushed his dagger into the midst of it as the bolo flew. The steel balls whipped around the blade on leather thongs, coming within an inch of Khyven's nose.

He turned and saw the man with a ridiculous unicorn helm. Unwieldy and tall, the whole thing was painted white-and-purple. The man lowered his head and charged like a bull.

Khyven flung the whole mess into his face.

Steel balls rang against painted steel, bashing into its eyes. The now blinded man stumbled past Khyven and fell to his knees.

It suddenly occurred to Khyven why all of these patrons kept attacking like a novice army, one at a time, poorly coordinated. They didn't *want* to attack him—with the possible exception of the smiling duelist. The mind control spell that had almost dominated Khyven—which he assumed Slayter had undone—was holding everyone else in thrall. They were attacking because they were being controlled ...

It's the card!

Slayter's statement finally clicked into place. The card was wreaking this havoc!

Khyven ducked underneath the bare-fisted strike of a burly man roughly Khyven's size. The man wore a leather X harness over his bare, bulging chest and a leather mask over his entire head, which left only a hole for his mouth and completely blocked out one of his eyes. The brawler tried to wrap his thickly muscled arm around Khyven's shoulders, but with all the strength in his legs, Khyven jumped up, driving his head into the man's jaw. The crack resounded throughout the tavern.

The big man stumbled back, trying to shake it off ... trying to shake it off ...

He fell onto his butt, then over onto his back.

Breathing hard, Khyven spun about to face the next attack—

But the entire tavern had gone still. The combatants stopped their advance, looking like querulous fronds in a breeze. Their brandished weapons slowly lowered.

Khyven shot a glance at the troll, who was back on his feet, face even more angrily crunched down than before. He glared at Khyven, but he didn't attack. He did lean forward, though, flexing his fist around that tree-sized club like someone was pulling on a leash around his neck.

Khyven glanced back at Slayter.

"... activated the Helm of Darkness. That was how he could control the creatures of the noktum. It was melting him, of course, mavric iron and all. But not for long. You see, he can wield Mavric iron. That's one of the delicious details I'll get to in a moment. It's a long story too, but part of this one. Oh, so many details. This may take a while—"

"Shut up," the card said. "Just stop talking."

"You brought us here for our story."

"A good story."

"Well, I've sketched out the rough elements. The details are far more—"

"You are the worst storyteller I've ever heard. It doesn't even fit together."

"I haven't filled in the details, but I promise I will. There are so many."

"No! You did it all wrong. Go stick a fork in your head."

"It's simply fascinating that you can speak." Slayter marveled. "Tell me one thing, and I promise to give you the rest of the story. Were you always a card? Are you a painting that was imbued with life? Or were you an imp that was ensorcelled into a painting?" Slayter reached for the card.

"Don't touch me. Don't touch—"

Slayter's fingers brushed the card. Blue light shot through the room like lightning.

The tavern vanished.

Waves of long grass extended in every direction except for the forest in the distance and the raised road that meandered toward it. Slayter's horse idly cropped the nearby grass. On the road, Hellface snorted and stamped a hoof.

Slayter turned two full revolutions, scanning the grass like he was expecting the tavern to be there. He finally stopped and sighed.

"Well, that's disappointing," he said.

"What is?" Khyven wiped the small bit of blood from the tip of his steel sword and sheathed it next to the Diplomat. "That you didn't get to watch me die for your amusement?"

"Watch you? I wasn't even looking at you."

"'Keep them busy?' Really?" Khyven snorted. "You owe me two daggers."

Slayter went to the place where he said he'd seen the "glowing card."

"Don't touch it!" Khyven grabbed his arm.

"Touch what?"

"The ... whatever! The card."

"Don't be silly. It isn't there anymore."

Khyven rolled his eyes. "Was it ever there in the first place? Or was this another one of your experiments that you didn't tell me about until we were in the middle of it?"

"What? Of course it was there."

Khyven waited while Slayter finished his thorough inspection, staying close enough that if he reached for anything, whether Khyven could see it or not, he was going to bodily pick up the slender mage and put him on his horse.

"It really was quite fascinating." Slayter limped over to his horse. Khyven stooped, laced his fingers together, and Slayter stepped into Khyven's hand with his good foot. Khyven helped the mage mount up, made sure he was secure before turning back to Hellface, who looked like he wanted a rematch.

They reached the road and, after a brief scuffle where Khyven got nipped on the knee and Hellface got socked in the nose, Khyven made it back into the saddle. He pulled hard on the reins to try to get the horse to stand still.

"So what did we learn?" Khyven growled.

"Not nearly enough. We barely had any time at all. It's tragic."

"Let me *tell* you what we learned. We learned that you don't just go touching magical cards to 'see what they'll do.'"

"You realize that was an entirely different dimension, right?"

"Like Daemanon? Where Nhevalos took Rhenn?"

Slayter sighed. "Daemanon is a continent."

"Then what is a dimension?"

Slayter seemed not to hear the question. "I don't think we'll ever get to go back there," he said ruefully.

"Promise?" Khyven growled, wheeling Hellface around and forcing him up the road.

"How can I possibly promise anything about which I have so little control?"

Khyven frowned. "You owe me two daggers."

"A promise like that requires far more information than I have, than I managed to get in the short span we were there. The details I'd need to recreate that dimensional teleportation spell is—"

"Slayter?" Khyven interrupted.

"Yes?"

"Shut up."

Atli the troll leaned against a table, the wood groaning under his solid weight. His ears rang and his head pounded. What the hell was that? Atli once fought and killed a pair of gold-tip bears with the broken haft of an oar, and after four hundred years his skin still showed the burn marks from single-handedly defeating a salt-blood warrior in its prime. But he had never encountered anything like the human who almost instantly beat him with a wooden sword and then left him flailing on the floor.

A human.

Hard-eyed fighters and street-smart toughs—those that thought themselves heroes—clambered to their feet to dust their clothes and wipe away blood. It almost seemed an insult the human with the false blade deigned not to kill any of them.

A breeze blew in through one smoking hole in the roof and out the second.

He cast a frown at Ild. How did the imp let this happen?

"They popped in on one of the extradimensional hooks," Ild said, his tiny painted shoulders shrugging beneath a depiction of a filthy undertunic. "Can't be sure what kinda yellow snow those'll bring in. The fighter had magic, and the magic one was an idiot."

"Sorcerer?" Atli's strong coastal accent carved the word from granite.

"No." Ild's long blue tongue hung out of his mouth to his knees, its forked tips twitching. "No sorcerers allowed. Something else." The painted imp looked across the room full of self-described heroes from his perch. Nothing more than an oversized playing card on the tavern's mantle. Bloodshot eyes narrowed within a smoke-stained wolf's head, and the grotesque rope of a tongue flickered over shiny black teeth.

"Now, who's next?"

The Jolly Chicken's front door creaked open, and a young Darrish woman, Egren nobility by her refined gold and red clothing, entered, a much paler-skinned Andosh man behind her. She wore a slender sword at her hip and a bow over her shoulder, while the man kept a simple dagger on his belt. His gray shirt with the short collar and dark blue vest identified him as Tyrranean.

A dusk heron lit on the edge of the western roof hole with a slight rustle.

"Latecomers here to tell more tales." Ild rubbed his black-clawed fingers together. "Siddown and wait your turn, goozy."

"I'm not here to tell stories," the young woman said. She stood unmoving by the door and surveyed the room. "I'm looking for ..." She stopped, cocked her head to one side, and stared at Ild. "I think we found what we're looking for."

Her companion nodded. "That's the power I felt. What's with all the hard-asses? This some kind of mean fucker convention?"

Atli strode forward, unlimbering his axe and trying to ignore the receding pain in his skull. "Yoo are here because Ild has summoned all in the lands who think they are heroes to tell their stories, yes? He vill be picking the one that can help him doing his own task and kill the rest." The troll indicated the last two empty chairs in the tavern with his axe. His ring mail jingled with the motion. "Sit and vait. It vill not be taking long. It never does."

"And why exactly would we do something so obviously skull-broke as that?" the Andosh man asked.

"You're going to kill these people?" As she spoke, the Darrish girl, pretty by human standards, pulled open her coat and rested her hand on the pommel of her blade.

Another problem. She should not be able to resist Ild's compulsion. The same spell that brought them here should enforce Atli's command over them. No one else ever shrugged off the imp's magic.

No one before today, that was. Now both these two, as well as the fighter and sorcerer before them proved immune. Atli could just kill the Darrish girl and her Andosh protector where they stood and move on, but why were they not doing as Ild commanded?

The imp apparently shared Atli's concerns.

"What d'you mean you're not here to share your heroics with me?" Ild asked. His body, that of a five-year-old boy with dead-looking gray skin, swayed from foot to foot. "Maybe you'd rather fall on that nice sword at your side?"

"No." The young woman's brow went up, confused. "And I'm no hero. We're here looking for a power that can help us."

"If you are looking for help, sit and vait your turn." Atli pointed at the chairs with his axe again, putting an extra measure of stone in his voice to show he meant business. He glanced again at Ild, who shrugged back at him.

"I'm not sitting there just so you can kill me after everyone tells you their stories," the woman said, matching Atli's stone with steel of her own. "And I'm not going to let you kill the others either."

Ild's voice rang out. "Atli, wait."

Atli lowered the axe he had been about to split the woman's head with.

"Help you what?" Ild's voice grew crafty. "And who are you?"

"Don't tell it anything." The Andosh man's gaze never left Atli's face, his dagger loose and unsheathed in his hand. "I don't know what we just walked into, but it's not fucking story time at the tavern."

"But you want to tell me your names, don't you?" the imp asked. He batted long eyelashes at them.

"I'm Masika. He's Rainn. That's Heron up there. She's with us." Masika pointed to the dusk heron that peered in the roof hole. The bird made a chirruping noise that sounded strangely like surprise.

"So you can be compelled." Ild tapped tiny claws against his lupine snout. "But you weren't when you got here. So why'd you make the trip to the Jolly Chicken, Masika, if it wasn't to regale me with your heroics? That's why the rest of these jackholes are here. I called anyone who thought they were a hero. But you apparently don't."

Before the man called Rainn could interject, Masika answered, "Rainn and Heron need help getting home from someone with power. You have power, so we came here."

"If yoo vant help, yoo must tell your story." Atli refused to let the evening get sidetracked again. These three—including the bird—only seemed unaffected by the compulsion because they did not consider themselves heroes and happened to walk in for reasons of their own. Now that

Ild understood, he could cast a new compulsion. But Atli thought that might not be necessary.

"I'll tell you our story." Masika's gaze darted between Atli, Ild, and Atli's axe. "But if I do, when this is all over, you have to let everyone else go. No killing."

A truly terrifying grin spread across Atli's face. Ild did not bargain.

"All right," Ild said, hanging open-mouthed surprise on the heels of Atli's grin. "But you go last. I want you to get to know everyone a little better before you screw the goat and everyone dies. You'll go down knowing that unlike the rest of these chair stains, you weren't spelled to tell your tale, and you got everyone killed all on your own."

"How do you know she's gonna fuck it up?" Rainn asked.

"Because I've been doing this for years." Black teeth glinted in Ild's smile. "This is the twentieth night across Andos like this Atli and I have hosted. All to find a hero capable of traveling to the Undergates and retrieving my creator, who was murdered before I could kill her myself."

Above them, Heron let out an angry squawk.

"I agree," Rainn said. He raised his dagger and pointed it at Atli's eye.

Every other bastard in the tavern stood, chairs screeching against the wooden floor, and pulled their weapons.

"Seems yoo have misjudged the room, yes?" Atli leaned over and plucked the dagger from Rainn's hand. "Now. Sit down and vait your fucking turn."

Masika and Rainn sat down.

Satisfied that control of the proceedings had been reestablished, Atli blew out a long sigh. "So, who is next?"

With a more subdued clatter of chairs and tables, all but one of the fighters, explorers, and at least one runecrafter sat back down. When they had, only a small Pavinn woman, youthful but knowing, remained on her feet.

She moved to the center of the room, faded green, blue, and yellow checks hemmed her patched skirt and marked her as Sedrian.

"My name is Edie," the young woman said, *"and my story begins on what any other girl would've considered the happiest night of her life."*

THE BLOSSOM QUEEN
C.M. MCGUIRE

It was the most beautiful time of year in the village of Gallraven, which was to say it was the time of year when the nearby swamp stank less than usual. Everyone who had the time and luxury to take a day away from their work capitalized on the season to gather as many wildflowers as possible, draping them in every door and window to further push back against the ever-present stink. This was accompanied by the grand spring festivities: competitions to eat unripe berries until somebody emptied their stomach, digging through the mud near the swamp for as many shellfish as possible and, of course, the spring tree dance.

Edie had never really belonged in Gallraven. She'd been found in a basket near the swamp and, however prettily she'd grown up, that reality clung to her like a lingering odor. But by whichever god spared her a thought, she could dance. If she put her mind to it, she could dance the stars into submission, much less her peers. And she was going to use that to improve her situation.

As the maidens of Gallraven gathered around the thick trunk of the Dancing Tree, Edie pressed on the flowers woven into her straw-colored hair, just making sure they were tight enough not to slip out. All the other girls wore their finest dresses, purchased from a swamp trader or made by their mothers. Edie smoothed out the wrinkles in her second-hand skirts. The Haddon family had been kind to give it to her, but it was old. The embroidery had worn down in some places, and the sleeves sagged down over her knuckles. Shabby as it was, it was the nicest a foundling milkmaid could hope for, and this was only the beginning for her. By this time next year, she was certain she'd have a dress twice as beautiful and made just for her.

All she had to do was out-dance all of them, and she'd have what she wanted.

The pipes started, and Edie jumped, grasping one of the ropes that hung from the thick tree branches. As one, each of the maids swung, kicking out until she landed on the patch of grass where the last maiden had been. And again, first one direction, then the other. As she danced, Edie spun, and the skirt flared out. Old as it was, old lady Haddon's dress had a hell of a skirt with a thick garland of ruffles at the bottom. Edie knew without even having to look down that, with each spin, Edie looked like a morning glory in bloom. She was springtime itself.

As the maidens spun, they all tried to lock eyes with Cedric, the Green King thanks to his ability to carry more baskets of berries than anyone else. And because his father was the magistrate. That counted for a lot more than a competition, after all. Edie grinned as his brown eyes locked with hers, a buzz of excitement shot through her. She was the one he'd been looking for this whole time. Edie leaped for the next rope and spun until the pipes stopped.

One girl yelped and slipped back into the dirt, staining her fine dress. But Edie held tight to the rope and lifted her chin. The men pretended to confer, but there was no cause to worry. At the end of the day, it was the Green King who chose the

Blossom Queen. All Edie had to do was dance well enough to convince everyone that the decision hadn't already been negotiated weeks before the festival. If she danced well enough, she could actually earn it. Cedric was already giving her an advantage. All Edie needed to do was disprove any naysayers who'd call the bluff. If she danced well enough, nobody would question why he'd chosen the strange milk maid with no parents.

Cedric stepped forward with a crown of woven branches and delicate, carved flowers worn by every Blossom Queen in the last decade. She bit her lip and leaned forward, toes in the dirt as she held tight to her rope. Cedric placed the crown on her head among all the wildflowers braided into her hair. At last, Edie heaved a deep sigh. She stepped forward, free of the mud, and finally released the rope. She'd done it. She'd promised him ages ago she'd do it, and she'd done it. A dismayed and subdued applause rose from the crowd like a disgruntled cat woken from its nap, but nobody protested. Edie had earned the honor after all.

"You know, everyone's going to expect us to get married, now," he whispered into her ear.

"Is that your proposal?"

"Oh no. My proposal will be far more public." He laughed. "I'll provide that house you always wanted."

Edie grinned, her stomach flipping as she glanced around. All eyes were on them. What did everyone think they were talking about? It was exciting, having people look at her and care about what she was doing. And none of them could possibly have any idea of the truth. If Edie was honest, she never would have learned the dance or bothered to participate if Cedric hadn't approached her with his idea. If he hadn't tempted her with something he knew she wanted so desperately.

"My own house," she said, her cheeks flushing. "Each of us with our own room."

"Room for us. For our lovers. For any other foundlings you want to take in." Cedric squeezed her hand. "My father won't question my romances if I marry the Blossom Queen."

"And nobody could look down on the wife of the magistrate's son."

In a town like Gallraven, some things were simply the way that they were. Young men had to marry young women so they could produce future young men and young women and keep on doing it to keep up the meager population. Foundlings were met with pity at best, suspicion on average, and resentment more often than Edie liked. To not want to make babies with a young man and to come from nobody-knew-where was as good as being the infamous swamp witch. Maybe Edie had more to gain but, either way, this was going to be salvation for both her and Cedric. They could both finally live the closest either of them could hope for to a good and respectable life in a shit town like Gallraven.

Edie looped her arm in Cedric's and proudly walked with him to the center of the town. All the other citizens of Gallraven, whether they liked it or not, followed. They had to. Even if they disapproved of their Blossom Queen, nobody was going to turn down the annual feast. Not even the young man who'd upchucked his unripe berries earlier in the day.

Edie clutched at Cedric's arm, more than happy to play the role of the swooning maiden. For his part, Cedric did an excellent job of keeping his eyes trained forward. He didn't even stray once to gaze at the butcher's son, even though they both knew he wanted to. There'd be plenty of time for that once the wedding vows were exchanged and they were settled in their nice, private house.

But, as they made their way to the head of the feast table, Edie felt a gaze on her that she did not care for. She tightened her grip on Cedric's arm, her smile slipping just a touch as they passed by a collection of rough-looking men. At the center of the pack stood Marnoc, the constable's brother. Marnoc spread his lips, scratching at the stubble of his beard as they passed, and Edie felt like she'd been slathered in tar just being close to him. She'd sooner kiss one of Mr. Haddon's dairy cows than let Marnoc touch her, not that he hadn't already tried.

"Don't worry," Cedric whispered. "He won't give us any trouble tonight."

"How are you sure?" Edie clenched her jaw. "He's tried plenty of times before."

"Because before you were alone. Tonight, you're with me. Once we announce our engagement, you'll have my whole family's protection."

Somehow, that didn't feel like it was going to be enough. Not when everyone knew the constable would simply sentence him to a night of sleeping it off in a cell, regardless of whether he'd stared at someone or stabbed them. When a man like him got to live above the law, it was never really possible to feel safe.

As the pink of dusk began to spread across the sky, Cedric and Edie took their seats at the head of the table. The rest of the village followed suit. Even Marnoc and his cronies sat at a table not far from their own, passing seed rolls and melon slices. But all the while, Edie could feel those eyes on her. Marnoc didn't eat a bite. He just ripped at a roll, his eyes straying to her again and again as he muttered under his breath to his men.

Edie scooted a little closer to Cedric, who made eyes across the table with the butcher's son.

"Wait until you have your own private room for that," she teased, but she couldn't keep the strain out of her voice as she reached for Cedric's wrist.

He turned to her immediately, twining his fingers with hers as he spared Marnoc a quick, tense glance.

"And what sort of activities will you enjoy in your room?" he asked. "How would you like me to have it built?"

If Edie was honest, she hadn't given it much thought beyond

the desire to have a room of her own. She knew Cedric's room would be a veritable inn for all the men of his own persuasion. Perhaps she would invite lovers of her own: lovely maidens or traveling merchant women. Male suitors had never excited her enough to budge her nickers. Maybe a woman would. Or maybe not. Maybe Edie would simply have her own bed and chest of drawers and writing desk and want to do nothing all day but sit by the window and read. As long as it was hers to do with as she pleased, in the comfort of a space she alone commanded, the activities that filled her free time didn't really matter. She just wanted better than a barn for a home.

She just wanted to feel safe.

"I can't eat with him watching me," Edie sighed. "Let's have a dance?"

Cedric nodded, stuffing a seed roll in his mouth before he rose and led Edie to the patch of ground surrounded by lanterns. The fiddler lifted his bow and, with the first hum of the strings, the first dance of spring began. One by one, more villagers joined in, hopping and spinning in a jig, and Edie felt safe in Cedric's arms, surrounded by a crowd.

Until the stench of cheap, half-turned wine filled the air.

Edie didn't have time to react before Cedric was shoved away, a familiar figure looming over her. She gasped, but Marnoc grabbed her wrists and dragged her close.

"Think you can nab yourself someone better than me?" Marnoc growled, pulling her flush against his chest.

Edie kicked and punched, but Marnoc had a good ten inches of height on her and far more muscle than that. Is the term "saltblood" or "salt-blood." I've got it two different ways here. Thank you!

"Get off her!" Cedric shouted, launching himself at Marnoc.

The constable's brother finally released Edie, and she fell to the ground in a heap, gasping. Marnoc and Cedric fell to the ground, rolling like wildcats in the dirt. In the fight, blood smeared over Cedric's face, gushing from a crooked nose.

"Get off him!" she cried, but she didn't know how to pull Marnoc off without taking a hit herself.

"Marnoc, what are you doing?" the constable shouted, and thank the gods he was an even bigger, beefier man than his brother. With the ease of a bird plucking a caterpillar off a branch, he ripped Marnoc off the now thoroughly bloodied Green King.

Mutters and whispers erupted through the crowd, and Edie's cheeks burned. How many other Blossom Queens could say they'd been the start of a fight at the festival? Never mind she hadn't wanted it. Never mind, if she had things her way, Marnoc would be rotting at the bottom of the swamp.

Cedric's mother knelt by his side, chastising him softly as she inspected his crooked nose and blackening eyes while his father, the magistrate, approached Edie stiffly.

"I suppose—" he cleared his throat. "With his intentions toward you ... if you'd prefer to come back to our house tonight ..."

But it was one of those invitations that wasn't really an invitation. It was the sort people suggesting midwinter celebrations around her extended—less because they wanted her there and more because they'd feel bad not inviting her. Cedric's nose had been broken all because Edie had taken his offer. Sure he'd get a wife who'd let him live as he pleased, but he was also going to get her troubles and dangers. She couldn't say whether or not his parents knew about him or that the two of them had been planning this for so long she'd had a whole season to practice the dance. But, even if they did, she wasn't family yet. She didn't belong with them yet. So they didn't actually owe her anything. Yet. Maybe never if Cedric had second thoughts.

"I think I'd just like to get some rest." She sighed, watching the magistrate and his men escorting Marnoc away. Would he be free again by morning? Certainly by the end of the week.

A few villagers halfheartedly tried to resume the dancing and feasting, but more than half gathered up the remainders of their meals in handkerchiefs and disappeared back to their homes. As far as Edie was concerned, the celebration was over.

As the first stars spread across the sky like spilled salt, Edie trudged back to the Haddon's barn, which was as close to home as she was going to get. At least, as close as she'd get until she and Cedric built a beautiful house where they could help each other to finally live private, beautiful lives. And yet, if Marnoc was willing to cause a scene like that in front of the whole village, could she really expect a marriage to do much more to deter him?

"Why me?" she muttered to herself, tugging the wooden crown from her head. Was it because she had no family and she seemed available? Or was it because there was actually something about who she was? Either way, it didn't much matter. Love or lust, Marnoc seemed determined to hound her and ruin any hope she had for a life of her own.

The further she wandered from the festival grounds, the closer she came to the swamp close to the Haddon farm. A swamp witch was supposed to live out there. Since Edie'd been found at the edge of the mud and muck, more than a few Gallraveners had assumed she was one such witch. Maybe she was. She certainly did have a talent for attracting trouble.

"If it is true, what trouble would I bring onto Cedric when I marry him?" she muttered. Suddenly, their plan felt less than ideal. If the hope was to seek out an alternative to happily ever after, then how happy could he really be if he kept having to fight off a madman seemingly immune to the law for the sake of a bride he didn't intend to bed?

"I wish someone would just cut off the bastard's head." Edie dropped the Blossom Queen's crown into the mud at the edge of the swamp and trudged up the hill overlooking the Haddon farm.

Her blood froze as shadows passed across the wide doorway of the barn.

Oh gods, she should have guessed. She should have seen it coming. Not one of Marnoc's petty cronies had attempted to shield him from arrest. Where else would they go but the very place where they knew Marnoc's target would head?

Edie ducked behind a bush, watching as the miscreants paced back and forth in front of the barn she called home. There were no lamps in the main house. The Haddons had to be lingering back at the festival. Good. They were safe. But they wouldn't be if they came home and Marnoc's men thought they could use them to get to Edie.

For a moment, she considered taking Cedric's father up on the shallow offer, but she pushed it down. Their son's nose had already been broken. How much more trouble did she dare bring upon one family in one night?

Edie sucked in a sharp breath. Maybe the constable was her chance. If she could prove his brother was using his friends as a small mercenary band to exert his will outside the law, then maybe, just maybe, the constable would do something about him. Something final.

And Edie could finally live a life of peace.

She turned and ran back toward the village, a crownless Blossom Queen in a threadbare, secondhand dress. A foundling without a true home of her own. A young woman without any breath but she ran until her lungs burned, her sides ached, until the fading lights of the empty festival grounds were past her and she came to the town central.

What could she say? What could she do to prove to the constable that his brother was a danger to Gallraven? Maybe hope was less foolish than the fruitless belief that Marnoc was truly beyond consequence. If she could convince the constable to come with her and spot the gang gathered at the Haddon farm, remind him that Marnoc'd broken the nose of the magistrate's son in front of the whole village. If the general misbehavior wasn't enough, if the harassment of a foundling milkmaid wasn't enough, then maybe this would finally lead to ... Well, she didn't know. If she was honest, she didn't want to think about it. She just wanted her home with her own room and the freedom to do and be whatever she liked.

She ran until her lungs threatened to burst, until she came to the constabulary. The door shook, then creaked open. Ice ran through Edie's veins. It wasn't the hulking form of the constable that lumbered out. She tried to suck in a breath, but she couldn't will her body to shiver enough to free her lungs.

Marnoc stumbled out the front door, his eyes glazed over. In one filthy hand, he clutched a dagger dripping red. He glanced around, looking suddenly like a kitten that couldn't find its mother. In a daze, he held up the knife before his eyes and shook his head, muttering something under his breath. Then he lifted his gaze, and two red-rimmed eyes latched on to Edie's.

"You," he croaked, pointing the dagger at her. "They were right about you, swamp witch."

"You killed your own brother," Edie breathed, staggering backward. Her head spun. Her ears rung. The constable was dead. The constable was dead and Marnoc was loose and absolutely nobody else was around to stop him.

Marnoc extended one shaky arm, his hand trembling so much the blood splattered off the blade like crimson raindrops.

"It was you," he croaked. "Since you came into your womanhood, you've hexed me. You've strung me about like a puppet. Couldn't think of anyone or anything else. And now you've driven me mad, haven't you? You made me do it. Swamp witch!"

"I won't be your excuse!" Edie shouted, glancing around wildly. But everyone was either at home or cleaning up the last dredges of the festival. Nobody to help. Nobody to restrain. He was twice her size and out of his mind with grief and lust. Edie wasn't going to stick around long enough to give him the opportunity.

She turned and ran, kicking up great clods of mud. Marnoc was armed and wild. She couldn't go to the magistrate. He might kill Cedric like he'd killed his own brother. She couldn't go to the Haddons. He might very well have his men burn the house down!

Well. If the bastards of Gallraven wanted to call her the foundling swamp witch, then she might as well embrace it.

She veered toward the source of the familiar reek at the edge of the village, launching herself out onto the wooden boards that meandered across the mud and cattails. The rotting slats creaked under her shoes, threatening to pitch her into the murky depths. With the stench of the swamp in her nose and the rising sound of swamp bugs in her ears, she couldn't tell how close Marnoc was, but she didn't dare stop to glance back.

For a brief, horrible moment, a thought occurred to her: what if she stumbled onto the actual swamp witch? There was a reason no Gallraven villagers dared to fish or forage in the swamp after dark, and why merchants only came their way during the day. And, in that brief, horrible moment, she couldn't help slowing down. What would the swamp witch do if she came upon her? Would she turn her into a fish or a frog or something worse? Would she cut her heart out and cook it in a stew? Was it going to be Edie's fate to spend her whole life being mistrusted and suspected of swamp witchery only to be killed by one? How did the merchants and peddlers that visited Gallraven navigate the crisscrossing paths without falling victim to the witch?

The thought only had enough time to form in her mind before the reverberation of footsteps shivered across the wooden planks. Well, better to fear the monster she knew than the monster she didn't.

So she ran. She ran even when a rotten plank sagged underfoot and threatened to send her leg plunging into the swamp. She ran even when her chest burned and her throat tightened and especially when she thought she could feel reverberations on the wood behind her and the fetid breath of Marnoc the monster. Even if it was in her mind, all she could do was run and run until the distant lights of Gallraven at night faded and the faint swamp lamps, almost half-burned by now, lit her path. Perhaps the lights would lead her to a rotten step. Perhaps she would plunge into the swamp and meet her fate at the jaws of some filthy creature caught between land and water. If it scared Marnoc off and kept Cedric and the Haddons from a lawless death, she might actually be grateful.

That thought alone was cause for alarm.

A building emerged, balanced on heavy stilts at the cross of two rotten and rickety boardwalks. Dull lamps glowed within the windows. That meant the building was occupied. But by whom? Nobody lived in these swamps, as far as Edie knew. As far as all of Gallraven knew. Nobody built a shelter or did business in this place except …

Well. Who better to protect a rumored swamp witch than an actual swamp witch?

Whether or not that was a good thing remained to be seen. If the whole of Gallraven weren't just superstitious sponge-skulls and this really was the home of the swamp witch, Edie might be able to convince her that she was a fellow witch. After all, she'd apparently done so to half of Gallraven without even trying.

Edie all but threw herself through the door, stumbling in the dark until she bumped into something. In the poor light of the window lamp, she could just make out a table with a mismatched assortment of chairs. If she wasn't certain this was a swamp witch's house, Edie might have been tempted to think she was in a pub or a tavern. What sort of lunatic would build one of those in the middle of a swamp?

No. There wasn't time to question the insanity of her circumstances. She needed to focus on surviving the night. Edie grabbed one of the chairs and shoved it up against the handle of the door.

"Hey!" a voice shouted. Edie whirled around, grabbing another one of the chairs–which turned out to be a stool–and brandished it in front of her. A woman stepped out from behind a long bar. Thick, wispy hair swirled around her freckled face like a black storm cloud.

Oh by the gods. Was this the swamp witch? Edie's breath caught in her throat as she raised the stool a little higher. She tried to think of something to spit out, but her throat tightened at the thought of all the horrible things a witch might turn a trespasser into.

The witch furrowed her brows and took a step forward. It must have been a bad step, though, because her foot slid underneath her and she went down, her face slamming into the edge of the bar.

What followed was such a slurry of pure and unrelenting vituperation that Edie was fairly certain her ears actually went a little bit numb. She blinked and lowered the stool just a hair as the witch slumped onto the floor, pinching the bridge of her nose. In the poor light, Edie could just make out the bright red of fresh blood.

"Did ... did you just hurt yourself?" she choked out. Maybe this wasn't a witch after all. Maybe this was a traveler taking shelter in a ramshackle building left to rot in the swamp.

The maybe-not-a-witch cracked open her eyes and lolled her head in Edie's direction. "Did you just barge in on planting night?" she slurred. "I'm closed on planting night."

"You're ...What?"

"I'm closed ...'cept for my nose. It's wide open." The not-a-witch groaned softly and gestured to Edie. "Fetch us a rag? There's bound to be one around here somewhere …"

Bam!

The slam of a heavy body against the door sent Edie screeching. She spun, hurling the stool at the door. It splintered into a pile of useless wood as the first chair stood firm. For the moment.

The not-a-witch moaned softly. "Tell us you weren't followed?"

"I-I'm running from someone." Edie squeaked, backing away from the door as Marnoc hurled himself at it a second time. All right. Time for a new plan. Playing by the village rules and finding a nice young man to protect her hadn't worked. Running hadn't worked. The only thing she had left was to fight. Maybe she was quicker than him. Smaller was supposed to mean quicker, wasn't it?

Edie snatched up one of the sharp chair legs and brandished it like a sword. If Marnoc was going to kill her for what he'd done, she'd be certain her final act in life would be to drag the bastard to death with her.

Hopefully.

At the very least she'd make things very, very difficult for him.

Behind her, the witch swore, but Edie didn't have the time to spare a thought for her or her involvement in this. The door slammed open, and Marnoc lumbered in, white spit frothed at the corner of his mouth as he wavered, raising up the bloody knife.

"You're gonna die, witch." He growled. "You're gonna die, and I'll finally be free of—"

There came a soft hiccup in the dark. Then a click. Edie froze. Marnoc grunted and glanced around sluggishly. He opened his mouth and …

A sound like a bursting pot crashed through the room as a

cool fog flooded down from the ceiling, its misty tendrils reaching for them. Edie stumbled back as Marnoc turned in a circle, his brows furrowed.

"What're you doing?" he demanded. "Stop it. I said stop it, witch!"

The sound of pans clattering and glass scraping was his response. A light shot through the room. Then another as a cackle, far too loud to have come from the drunk not-witch earlier, boomed off the walls and tables and through the smoky air.

"You've stepped through the wrong door," the voice said. "Time for you to learn just what a swamp witch is really capable of."

All right. Maybe she really was a witch.

"That's enough!" Marnoc bellowed, jabbing the knife into the air and spinning slowly. The threat Edie had posed must have completely fled his mind as he searched for the seemingly invisible woman. It was all at once horribly intimidating and pathetic, this drunken tree trunk of a man searching the dark. His hand trembled. The same blood-covered hand that he'd used to stab his brother.

Edie lunched forward, smacking the back of his head with all her might. There was an awful *thunk* and a wheeze like all the air had been pushed from him at once. Marnoc staggered forward then turned, staring down at Edie with unfocused eyes.

"Witch," he sputtered, but before he could jab the knife at her, she swung the stool leg a second time, this time with the satisfying crack of his jaw flipping free from the joint. Spittle and blood dribbled from his mouth as he sagged down and, at last, dropped the knife right before his head hit the floor.

Edie snatched up the knife and brandished it in front of her, just in case Marnoc came to and decided to jump at her again, but all he seemed capable of doing was drooling and bleeding into the smoke, which had already begun to dissipate.

"Hope you're happy," the woman said, and Edie spared her a quick glance. The woman, walked out of a door Edie hadn't noticed before, carrying a basket of what looked like pots, pans, and white-dusted bits of pottery. She dropped the box on top of the bar and wiped at her bloody nose with a scowl. "It'll be days to set all that up again. I hope that smelly old lump was worth the show."

"He ... he killed his brother. The constable," Edie said faintly. "And he broke my fiancé's nose. My almost fiancé. My fiancé in waiting." Well, probably not even that anymore.

"Seems to be catching," the woman said, gesturing at her face. "So. I take it he's a right bastard that's better off being fed to the swamp."

Edie blinked, then glanced down at Marnoc, then back up at the woman. "Who are you?"

"I'm the Swamp Witch," the woman said, leaning against the bar. "Well. That's what some of the little shit-for-shingles villages call me. Probably where you're from. Where is that exactly? Cairnen? Elmbrik?"

"Gallraven."

The woman snorted, then winced. "Gallraven. Of course they'd produce a specimen like that man. You're the first Gallravener to come out this far. Your lot are usually too superstitious to set foot outside that little fart of a village."

"So ... so you're not a witch?"

"Depends on the definition of witch." She arched a brow. "Would you consider an enterprising woman who knows how to put on a show to spook off ne'er-do-wells to be a witch?"

It took a moment for the reality of the situation to piece through the cloud of fear that had been Edie's mind since she saw the men at Haddon farm.

In her terror, she'd run right into the lair of the swamp witch. On purpose. And Marnoc had followed her, and she'd just managed to take him down because the swamp witch helped her. Only she wasn't a witch at all. The mist. The crash. It must have had something to do with the broken bits of pottery. The clanging was the pots and pans. She must have had another trick around somewhere to make her voice boom the way it had.

"What is this place?" Edie breathed.

The woman glanced around and, with a grin, gestured at the wide room. With her eyes finally adjusting to the poor light and the smoke clearing, Edie could make out half a dozen tables scattered across a room constructed of what must have been a dozen different types of wood, the refuse of carts and houses and even some of the planks from the walkway across the swamp. Lanterns hung from the walls, unlit and interspersed with the odd animal skull or scribble of art on a bit of wood and hammered in place. Across one wall stood a low stage, the wood scuffed and worn.

"This is my bar," she announced. "Bought it off a fisherman a couple of years back. I've been trying to turn it into something nice. I call it Pick's Pocket. And I'm Pickett." She held out a hand smeared with white dust and dried blood.

Dazed, Edie took it. "Bar? You mean an inn?"

"Pfft! I don't rent out rooms. Closer to a pub, I suppose. Maybe a tavern if I'm generous. I sell food and drink, mostly drink, and I'm a trading stop for travelers, but I'll not have them sleeping in the same place I do."

"Is that why you trick them into thinking you're a witch? To keep them away?"

Pickett shrugged. "I put on a show and let them draw their own conclusions. If I'm honest, this is the first time I had to do it to stop someone from getting gutted."

"Oh. Yes. Thank you for that." Edie glanced back at Marnoc. "Do you think he'll survive the night?"

Pickett arched a brow. "Do you want him to?"

Did she? It was a fair question. After everything he'd done, everything he'd proven he would do, she wouldn't be safe if he lived. But he was also a living person, and one she'd hurt badly. Every second that he didn't rise from the floor worsened the risk that he might never rise the same way again. He might spend the rest of his life in a haze, his brain broken by Edie's blow.

In which case, it would be a mercy killing, really.

"What'd you say about feeding him to the swamp?"

Pickett grinned, and in the poor light, covered in her own blood, she really did look like a witch. "I'll fetch some rope."

Marnoc only began twitching once they dragged him out onto the splintery walkway outside of the bar, his hands and feet bound behind him like a backwards hog. Edie suspected had a splinter not lodged itself into his cheek, he might have drifted contentedly into a head wound-induced oblivion. As it was, he stared sluggish up at them, growing increasingly aware with each second. He grunted in pain and tried to say something, but only managed to drool out some more blood.

"On three," Pickett said. "One—"

But Edie wasn't interested in waiting that long. She shoved Marnoc as hard as she could, tipping his large body into the murky water. There was thrashing and some bubbles—sounds that might have been cries or oaths gurgled up with the bubbles. Eventually, she'd probably have to sit down and think about the uneasy weight of that in her stomach, but she wasn't in the mood at the moment. She was tired and filthy and he was gone. That was all she really cared about.

"I heard somewhere that dead bodies float," she said, glancing at Pickett. "Should we be worried?"

"What's left of him will float but I doubt there'll be much once the swamp beasties are through with him." Pickett shrugged and gave Edie a nudge. "He's certainly not going to follow you back to Gallraven."

"I suppose," Edie muttered. Deep down, she couldn't help suspecting that was exactly what would happen. Marnoc makes a bold move on the foundling girl. Breaks the nose of her Green King. The Haddocs are terrorized by Marnoc's men. The next thing anyone knew the constable was dead, Marnoc was missing, and Edie appears apparently unscathed. Did she kill him? Did she kill his brother? Did she use some wicked magic and go back to her milking or marrying the magistrate's son? No. If something wicked happened, it would come back to her. She could have been asleep every second since the festival and they wouldn't care. She was a strange foundling girl. It would always come back to her.

She sank down, her throat burning as she watched the odd bubble float upward. "It's only a matter of time until they decide they're more scared of me than they ever were of him. They've always been afraid. Gallraven doesn't like foundlings."

"Mm. They probably think you're a half-demon spawn or—"

"Swamp witch, actually." Edie glanced up at Pickett with a wry smile. "Funny I was saved by one."

"You're the one who smashed in his skull," Pickett pointed out, arching her brow. "Not that it'll help you, I'm sure."

Edie sighed and pushed herself to her feet. "I was planning to marry someone who could protect me, but once people decide I turned Marnoc into a fish and ate him or some such, I'll only bring trouble onto Cedric and his whole family."

"Spoken like someone madly in love."

Edie laughed. "If I'm honest, I've never really been inclined toward love. Cedric and I had an understanding."

Realization dawned on Pickett's face as her mouth formed a perfect O. Then she grinned. "So I take it you're not actually so keen to marry him. Clearly you aren't keen to go back to that town. And I'm just sober enough, now, to offer you a job." She jerked a thumb over her shoulder. "You've got until I open another bottle to make up your—"

"Yes!" Edie blurted before her mind could catch up with her mouth. And once it did, her heart swelled up so big it could hardly fit in her chest. A job in a bar in the middle of a swamp may not sound as comfortable as being a milkmaid, but it would be with someone who didn't bat an eye at a foundling. Who'd blown all her defenses for a stranger within minutes of meeting her. Nothing in Gallraven would compare.

Pickett threw back her head and let out a loud laugh as she wrapped an arm around Edie's shoulders. "Good. Because you need to work to pay me back for that stool. I'll get you started first thing in the morning. For now, let's get a drink."

Edie couldn't stop herself from smiling as she walked with Pickett back to the bar. A safe haven, at least for the moment.

Damn. Atli hated stories like that. People who survived terrible circumstances, who might even be right to consider themselves heroic, but who could never face the kinds of trials Ild intended to throw at them. It was a shame, because if some well-meaning fool in this girl's life had not told her what a hero she was—and made her believe it—Ild's spell of compulsion would never have caught her, and she wouldn't be here.

From his place on the mantle, Ild dropped his wolfen head into one clawed little hand and sighed.

Atli slumped. He knew this sort of wasted time pissed the imp off.

"Sorry, Edie." Atli touched a forefinger to the steel-shod tip of one of his horns. "It's not yoo. Ve are looking for someone vith bigger potential, yes? Yoo can sit back down."

To Atli's left, a man stood, his Pavinn face screwed up in distaste.

"No, I won't eat that"—he pointed to a small pile of red gel-covered balls on his tabletop being offered by a woman his age—"and I can tell the story myself. You're so hungry, you eat them while I talk." So saying, he stalked to the center of the room and crossed his arms.

"Tyrac here," he began, "and you're not going to believe this. Anyone here ever heard of Pallid?"

LOCAL CUISINE
ETHAN A. COOPER

1 Before a meal, speak quiet prayers to the twin gods.

2 Give thanks to your father Kak for the nourishment that the meal provides but plead with your mother Viv that the meal will not consume your bowels.

- Communions and Supplications 67:1-2, The Book of Kak

Sneaking out of the wooded city of Pallid unnoticed in the morning should have been difficult for a priestess of the Kin, but it was easy enough for Leila when Tyrac was with her, which he always was.

"I can't believe I let you talk me into this again," Tyrac said when they were well past where the perimeter guards would patrol. He pushed his green hood back, adjusting the waterskin and supply pack slung across his chest.

"You say that every time we come out here," Leila said.

"It's always true. You know one of these excursions is going to get me killed, right?"

Leila smiled as she passed. Her face when she smiled was

like the midday sun. Tyrac felt that if he looked at it too long, it'd be the last thing he'd ever see. She'd always had this sort of effect on him, even when they were kids.

Tyrac fell into step beside her and sighed. Normally, they'd continue this line of banter for a good half hour, but he had other plans for this particular trip. There were more important words to say to her when the time was right.

The Wood of Night Sins was thick with peril, but their confidence was increasing. They strayed farther from the safety of Pallid with every trip.

Leila stopped, as she often did, to bend down and harvest something from the ground. Her black hair, which she never constrained, stretched to the ground like the branches of a wild willow. The satchel slung across her torso swung forward, causing the sigil set into its surface to glint in a shaft of sunlight. The vials on her belt clinked together like bells, adding strange new notes to the song of the woods. Birds singing, wind drifting through leaves, and in the distance, the sharp snapping of twigs.

"Those look delicious," Tyrac said, bending down beside her. "You cooking those for dinner tonight?"

Leila laughed, holding up the mushrooms she'd picked. "Only if we're planning on it being our last meal. Eat these and you'll bleed from every orifice you know about, plus a couple more you don't."

"Wonderful. And you have a whole fistful of them."

"A girl has needs."

Another twig snapped. Whoever it was, they were closer, and they were clumsy.

Tyrac drew a small throwing knife from its sheath under the leather wraps on his forearm, making sure Leila saw him do it. He raised his hood and lifted his mask up over his nose.

Leila placed the mushrooms in her satchel and pulled a small red pouch from her belt. Tyrac couldn't keep track of all the various concoctions she carried, but the contents of that pouch were sure to be unpleasant.

"I'm sorry," Leila said. "It's my fault. I missed something."

"It was only a matter of time," Tyrac said, barely able to keep his frustration at the situation from affecting his voice.

When Tyrac nodded, Leila ran onward. Tyrac darted back in the direction of the stranger. He could see them crouched behind the splintered trunk of a fallen tree. Tyrac was hesitant to give a potential opponent one of his weapons, but he sent his knife flying anyway. It hit the fallen tree with a sour *clang* and went skittering into the underbrush. Tyrac approached at a full run. The stranger, who was shorter than Tyrac had expected, stood and turned to find Leila waiting for him, the hand with the red pouch at her back.

"How did you get over here so fast?" Tyrac asked.

Leila said, "I took a shortcut."

The stranger was a teenage boy, standing there with crossed arms and set jaw. His dark hair fell over his ears and fell into his eyes. He wore a brown traveling cloak over simple attire but didn't appear to be carrying much. There was a small knife on his belt, which meant he was from Pallid. All members of the Kin carried a shiv, but most didn't display it so prominently.

"Wherever you're going, you're taking me with you," the boy said.

"And if we don't, you'll tell somebody about what we're doing," Tyrac said. "Is that it?"

The boy sneered. "Just think about what will happen to her if the Hallowed discover what their favorite priestess has been doing. And what about you? You're an Illumined. A city guard who's not guarding his city."

"What's your name, boy?" Tyrac asked. "What's your rank? Show me your mark."

Leila put a hand on the boy's shoulder. "We don't need to see his mark. He's an acolyte of the Kin, and his name is Grif."

Though he should have been scared, Grif appeared to be impressed that a priestess knew who he was.

Leila continued, "Grif here is the eldest son of Ged. You know who Ged is. The king's most-trusted adviser."

"My father is a very important person," Grif said.

"He is," Leila agreed, her hand still on his shoulder.

"One word to my father could cause a lot of trouble for you."

"It could."

Tyrac bent to retrieve his knife from the ground. He briefly considered knocking the kid out and dragging him back to Pallid. They'd leave him where a patrol could find him before some animal could. "Why did you come out here, kid?"

"For the same reason you're out here. Pallid is boring. You're taking me with you, and that's final," Grif said.

"Pallid isn't boring," Leila said, "but the Wood of Night Sins is a dangerous place."

"You won't let anything happen to me."

"Stay right here while Tyrac and I discuss your proposal," Leila said. She brought the red pouch directly in front of Grif's face. The surface of the pouch bulged outward briefly. "If you move, you're going to find out what genital worms do to genitals. Despite the way it sounds, it's not pleasant."

Leila and Tyrac moved out of hearing range, leaving Grif to do his best impersonation of a statue.

"How old is this kid?" Tyrac asked, removing his hood and mask, and running fingers through his short, curling hair. He kept it trimmed to deny his sparring opponents from using it against him. He'd considered growing it out, but Leila had made a casual comment at some point that she liked his hair short.

Leila leaned close so she could keep her voice low. "He's thirteen. Oldest of three. Lis and Stev, his younger siblings are twins. They're seven. They're going to grow up to be just like him, and he's just like his father."

"What do you want to do?" Tyrac asked. He already knew the

kid was coming with them, and that he wasn't going to fight her, but he wanted her to say it out loud. "Nobody knows we're out here except him. I know a couple of places to hide a body."

"Really? You've been holding out on me. Let's take him with us and make sure something out here scares him so bad that it's the last time he tries to blackmail anybody."

"You have some ideas for how to do that?"

Leila nodded, her eyes as wicked as he'd ever seen. "And if none of those work, there's always the worms."

Tyrac whispered, his breath tickling her ear. "Tonight, when the kid's asleep, I have something I want to talk about."

"Sounds serious. Am I in trouble?"

"Since the very first moment we met."

He didn't give her a chance to respond, pulling her toward Grif.

"All right, kid, you can come," Tyrac said, doing his best to avoid looking at Leila. She either had a good idea what he wanted to discuss, or she'd be wondering throughout the day. Tyrac wasn't sure which scenario he preferred.

"This is a one-time arrangement," Leila said. "We'll be out here today and tomorrow. When we return to Pallid, you keep our secret, and I keep the worms in their pouch where they belong. Do you agree?"

"Yes," Grif said

"Good. We will finalize our agreement with a second-degree oath ritual."

Leila inscribed an intricate triangle design in the dirt. Each of them stood at a corner. She took a vial of yellow liquid from her belt, removed the stopper, and poured a couple of thick, syrupy drops into each of their palms. Grif scrunched his nose up at the liquid's acrid odor. Returning the vial to her belt, she instructed the three of them to join hands. Nobody disobeyed a priestess's instructions during a ritual.

"*The oath breaks, the flesh rots,*" Leila said. "Say it."

Tyrac had never taken a second-degree oath before, and it was clear from the way Grif's eyes went wide, he hadn't either. But there was no backing out. They repeated her words.

"It is done. For obvious reasons, don't break your oath." Leila let Grif's hand drop but held onto Tyrac's.

"This stuff smells like urine," Grif said.

"I'm sure it is," Tyrac said. Leila's knowledge of ingredients for rituals was unmatched among priestesses of the Kin. She usually had a wide assortment of bodily fluids from a wide assortment of creatures on her person. It could get quite smelly.

"Oh, it's *much* worse than that," Leila said, squeezing Tyrac's hand, aggressively working the fluid in. She addressed Grif. "You want to explore the woods with us and avoid being disemboweled by a wood wraith? Then do everything we tell you without question."

"Where are we going?" Grif asked. His voice had picked up a slight waver, probably at the mention of the wood wraith, which Tyrac was *almost* sure Leila had made up.

"You ask too many questions," Tyrac said.

"We're finding something to eat," Leila said. "Some local cuisine."

Grif blew out a breath but followed when Leila started walking. "This had better be more interesting than it sounds. Eating is boring."

"Did you bring any food with you?" Tyrac asked.

Grif paused, his defiant expression revealing the answer.

"Then finding food will be a lot more interesting soon."

Over the next several hours, Leila offered Grif a smörgåsbord of the wood's delicacies. He declined to sample the fistful of plump beetles she extracted from underneath a mossy stone, even after she popped one in her mouth and slowly bit down on it. When she scooped some rainbow lichen from the surface of a small pool of rainwater, she gnawed off a chunk and offered him half. He shook his head. They found a family of sap suckers attached to the base of a tree, their bulbous sap sacs swollen to almost bursting. Leila said a quick prayer, then slit the back of one, catching the ooze in one of her vials. She took a swig, but before she capped the vial and placed it back on her belt, she held it out to Grif. He held up a hand to ward her off and looked as if he might vomit.

"I know what you're doing, and it's not going to work," Grif said.

"There's nobody here to bring your supper," Tyrac said. "Out here, we live off the land."

"I didn't see you eating any of what she's eating."

"And you never will."

Grif hadn't noticed, but Tyrac had been eating regularly out of his own supplies. While he wasn't going to offer the kid food, Tyrac also didn't want him passing out, so he shared his waterskin several times, Leila staring at him with open amusement.

Tyrac continued to defer to Leila's course. As had been their original plan, she led them into a portion of the wood they hadn't explored previously. The land began to slope, the trees growing closer. Leila paused every so often to sketch the landscape on her ever-expanding map. In addition, Tyrac was diligent in marking trees along the way. He had a decent sense of direction, and Leila had her map, but he liked to be prepared for all scenarios. A person could get turned around. Maps could be lost.

The afternoon wore on.

Tyrac was about to suggest that they stop for the day when Grif pointed and said, "There's a sign up ahead."

Sure enough, mostly obscured by drooping branches, there was a ragged plank of wood nailed to a tree. The kid was an entitled, manipulative runt, but he had excellent eyesight.

"Also, I'm hungry," Grif said.

Tyrac didn't sense anybody in the immediate area, so he led them forward.

"That sign is really low," Leila said.

The sign was about a meter off the ground. It read *ewar avenou hildre* in crooked letters formed of broken twigs.

"Do you recognize the language?" Tyrac asked. The library in Pallid was like a second home to Leila.

"No," Leila said. "Maybe it's a code. Or maybe there are letters missing. What do you want to do?"

Be out here alone with you, were the words Tyrac wanted to say but didn't. "We'll have to go back the way we came before we make camp."

"Don't you want to see if we can find who made the sign?"

"We're not allowed to talk to outsiders," Grif said.

Leila turned on him. "And you're not allowed outside the walls of Pallid. You forget your rank again, *acolyte*. Firstborn son of the king's adviser or not, don't lecture me on the laws of the Kin again. Remember, this is what you wanted."

Tyrac said, "We can't risk staying here or going further. Not with the kid."

Leila moved closer and lowered her voice. "We need to scare—"

Somewhere in the woods, but entirely too close, a child giggled.

At that sound, Leila uttered a curse word expressly forbidden by chapter seven, verse eighty-nine of the Principles and Prohibitions section of the *Book of Kak*.

Grif ran so that he was positioned between Leila and Tyrac.

A young girl of no more than ten years emerged from behind a bush. Her face was dirty, and the braid in her black hair was askew, as if she'd been playing in the woods all day. She wore a plain gray tunic tied with a brown cord.

"Was she there all along, or did she sneak up on us?" Leila asked.

Tyrac knew what she was really asking was, *How did you not know she was there, Tyrac?*

"Hello," the girl said. "My name is Ama. What are your names? What are you doing here in our forest? Are you lost? Are you a family? Is that your wife? She's pretty. You're tall. Is that your son? How old is he? Did you bring food? Are you hungry? I heard your son say he was hungry. If you're hungry, you can follow me. My sister makes the best soup. She works at the Tasty Goat. C'mon!"

Having said all that in one breath, the girl turned and skipped away.

"No," Tyrac said when he saw the look on Leila's face.

"Don't deny me, Tyrac. Stay here with the boy while I get a taste of the local cuisine."

"I'm not staying with him," Grif said.

"They're outsiders," Tyrac said. "I thought you didn't want to talk to outsiders."

"Outsiders with food. I'm starving."

Tyrac pulled Leila away. "This could be much worse than us sneaking out of the city. I know you like new experiences, but we've talked about this before. We agreed we would avoid outsiders."

"Grif being with us changes things," Leila said. "He's the real risk. The oath isn't going to be enough to keep him from talking. We have to push him further if we want to be safe. He needs to be mired in sin, deep enough that the consequences are too dire to even ponder."

"More dire than rotting flesh? Anyway, what about us? What about our sins? What we're doing is worse. We're causing him to commit offense."

"We'll perform a sacrifice and a purge. The twin gods will forgive us."

Tyrac didn't know whether that was true or not, but he did know that he wasn't able to deny Leila, even when she was about to violate a prime tenet of the Kin.

"Tonight, after we're all done sinning, sacrificing, purging, and whatever else it takes to atone for our misdeeds, you and I are going to have our talk," Tyrac said. At that point, he didn't care if Grif could hear every word he'd say to her. He turned away before he could get any angrier at himself, at the sway she held over him.

"I knew it. I am in trouble."

She was smiling as she said it. Tyrac could hear it in her voice.

He moved in the direction the girl had gone. When he passed Grif he muttered, "Stay close to Leila. If anything happens to me, she'll get you home."

If Tyrac's words had evoked any fear into Grif, the boy hid it well, falling into line and continuing to grumble about how hungry he was.

As it turned out, Ama was waiting for them to catch up. When she saw them approach, she giggled and moved on again, gesturing for them to follow. She repeated this cycle of rushing ahead and waiting patiently until they were close enough to spot her. There didn't appear to be any consistency to the course she took through the trees, and there was no discernible path on the ground. Tyrac continued to mark trees using the system he and Leila developed. Leila scrawled lines on her map as best she could while moving.

They descended into a valley. Eventually, there was a narrow path in the dirt, which Ama skipped along as they followed.

Grif did stay close to Leila as instructed, crowding her like a son might his mother. She didn't push him away.

The path widened, and they came to the outskirts of a settlement. There were crude, wooden structures built with hewn logs, in many ways not so different than those in Pallid. However, unlike Pallid, these structures seemed to be set among the trees in a disorganized manner, as if somebody had just thrown stones into the woods to determine where they should build.

Dusk had not yet come, but torches had already been lit.

There was a healthy amount of movement in the settlement: fires being tended, shouting and laughing, little children playing.

There was no gate barring their entrance, though there was a guard on either side of the path, each wielding a pike with a long multi-colored shaft and tipped with a ragged metal tip. The guards, faces shrouded by hoods and scarves, were over two meters tall and wore long green cloaks that fell all the way to the ground. The material of the cloak moved, as if being touched by a wind that affected nothing else. None of the outsiders Tyrac or Leila had seen on their previous illicit ventures into the woods or within Pallid's walls had been as tall as these two.

Ama skipped between the two guards as if they weren't there.

The guards crossed their pikes across the path.

"Let them in," Ama whined. "They're my new friends, and they're hungry."

Leila stepped forward. "We only seek a hot meal at the Tasty Goat."

She didn't seem nervous about talking to outsiders. Tyrac supposed it was the same as talking to Kin, just more forbidden by their culture. If Leila had talked to any outsiders who were detained when they occasionally wandered close to Pallid, she hadn't ever mentioned it to him.

At Leila's explanation, the guards lifted their pikes and allowed them to continue.

Ama ran back to Leila, grabbed her hand, and pulled her along. "This way!"

The residents ignored the newcomers for the most part. Tyrac caught quick glances from youthful faces before they would turn back to their task. Some of the children opened their mouths in surprise and pointed.

Tyrac counted twenty buildings, most of them houses,

nestled within the trees. There were rock formations scattered around as well. The vegetation had overgrown most of them, so they blended in with the surrounding wooded landscape. The largest rock formation was tall enough that it nearly reached the treetops. At its base was a structure of tree branches, curved over and bound together to form a hallway that led directly into the rock. Lashed to the sides of the structure were effigies constructed of carved branches and colored thread. Two guards stood motionless at the threshold.

Farther on, the ground leveled out, and an area had been cleared to facilitate larger gatherings. Simple benches made of split logs surrounded a ring of rocks that were black with soot. Three youths, no older than Grif, chased each other around the benches.

Just off to one side was a larger, carefully constructed structure. Its high walls and steep roof were made of wood planks, and it had a covered porch. The sign hanging from the edge of the roof was slightly askew but had neat lettering, as if the sign maker took pride in their work and the person who'd hung the sign didn't. On the roof, smoke wafted from a small chimney.

"Here it is. The Tasty Goat!" Ama announced with a dramatic flourish, letting go of Leila's hand only to grab Grif's. "Want to be my new big brother? The one I have is really dumb."

Grif yanked his hand out of her grasp, but Ama remained staring up at him in awe.

The three youths playing around the fire pit came over and crowded around Grif, touching his clothes and peppering him with questions. *What's your name? How old are you? Are those your parents?* The questions came so fast he hadn't answered any of them.

"Looks like the kid is popular with outsiders," Tyrac said.

Leila studied their surroundings. "The world is a curious and confusing place. I'm trying to understand it, though I don't think I ever will."

"Aren't you supposed to be getting us something to eat?" Grif said loudly, having to talk above the barrage of questions being launched at him. More children in the area had taken notice and were on their way to see what all the excitement was about.

"Be nice to them," Leila said.

"I'll be nice once I get something in my belly that wasn't growing on the bottom of a rock or drooled out of some animal's mouth." Grif stepped up on one of the benches and was quickly surrounded on all sides. "Uh, it's getting dark soon. Shouldn't you all be in your homes? Where are your parents?"

Tyrac actually had the same question. Outside of the guards, he hadn't seen anybody that could have been older than Leila, and she was nineteen.

Grif tried to step off the bench, but his admirers protested. *Let your parents go in without you. Stay out here and play with us. You'll be bored in there.*

Tyrac made no move to help him, but said, "Let's go, Grif."

Leila paused at the door to the Tasty Goat. "Yes, come along, Son." She actually giggled when she said that last word.

Tyrac did not mind that sound at all.

Grif pushed through the children to a barrage of vociferous protests. He ran past Tyrac and followed Leila inside.

The children kept their distance from Tyrac, but they crowded around the Tasty Goat as he entered.

He let the door swing shut behind him. The room was lit with candles placed around the room. There was a cooking pot in a stone hearth to one side, a single round table with three chairs in the center, and a counter at the far end of the room. The place was clean, filled with earthy smells: dirt, herbs, flowers, and whatever was bubbling in that pot.

In addition to Leila and Grif, there were three other persons inside. Two guards stationed on either side of the door, and a cheerful girl behind the counter. She wore a gray bandanna around her neck, a white apron over a brown tunic, and a smile that invited them right in. The girl wasn't a day over fifteen.

Tyrac motioned for Grif to go sit down at the table. Instead, Grif stepped closer to Leila.

"Welcome to the Tasty Goat," the girl said. "What can I get for you?"

"Your sister Ama said you make soup. I'd like to trade for three bowls." Leila extracted a pouch from her satchel, placed it on the counter, and pulled on the strings holding it closed. "Herbs and spices from my home. They're fresh. Foraged everything myself. Ground and mixed them yesterday."

The girl's eyes perked up when she sniffed the contents of the pouch. She placed the pouch on a shelf behind her, pulled three bowls from under the counter, and walked over to her cooking pot.

"My soup's the best around. You won't find anything else like it in this part of the woods." She winked at Leila as she returned with full bowls. "Lots of special ingredients."

The soup smelled sweet and comforting. Small bits of meat and vegetables floated in an amber base. It made Tyrac think of Pallid. He eyed the door and the guards on either side. He wished he could see their faces, but the length of their hoods made that impossible.

The girl behind the counter was watching Leila with no small amount of expectation, like a daughter seeking her mother's approval.

One of the guards turned their head to look at Grif. The movement caused their cloak to swing open, giving Tyrac a quick peek underneath.

Leila hadn't been provided a spoon, so she used both hands to lift one of the bowls to her mouth. The hot liquid had barely touched her lips when the heat of Tyrac's body blasted against

57

her as he came up behind and grabbed both of her wrists. Leila had *almost* tasted the soup.

Tyrac's lips were hard against her ear. "Even you don't want to eat whatever's in that. Also, each guard behind us is actually just two kids pretending to be an adult. One is just sitting on top of the other's shoulders. Something is very wrong here. We're leaving."

Leila dropped the bowl. It slammed into one of the other bowls, catapulting hot soup into the face of the girl behind the counter. She screamed, clutching her face.

Tyrac spun Leila around, threw a hand over her shoulder, grabbed Grif, and moved them all toward the door.

The guards had thrown their cloaks back to reveal that they were indeed each a younger child perched on the shoulders of an older teenager. While the stronger teenagers held their pikes crossed to block the exit, the children on their shoulders raised clenched fists.

Tyrac shoved Leila and Grif back as he reached for his knives. He'd avoid inflicting serious injury if he could. Children were sacred to the Kin. They were not to be harmed.

But these weren't Kin.

There was movement in his peripheral vision followed by sudden, sharp pain in his forearm. The girl behind the counter was no longer behind the counter. Her teeth, if fact, were buried in Tyrac's arm.

Despite the pain, he resisted the urge to flinch away, instead he shoved two fingers on the girl's philtrum, then pressed up, sending both fingers up her nose. Reflexively, she recoiled, her teeth trailing blood as she went. Tyrac pressed his advantage with a shout and a strike to the side of her neck. Her eyes fluttered as she went down, crashing into the table before collapsing to the floor. He hadn't hit her hard enough to collapse her windpipe, but she wasn't going to get back up any time soon. Sprawled there on the floor, the skin on her face an angry red from the soup, she pulled at her bandanna, but it didn't look like she could get her fingers to work properly.

Leila uttered a particularly offensive expletive, followed by, "Tyrac!"

Tyrac's instincts told him to duck, which he did, though it didn't save him from getting hit with whatever it was that the top half of the guard on the right had thrown at him. The unidentified object caught him right in the mouth. It burst, sending a thick, green substance all over the place. He coughed, feeling the stuff sour against his tongue.

Beside him, Leila grunted as she too was hit. She wiped away the goop from her eyes, one hand frantically searching through her satchel.

Grif, who had backed away toward the hearth, appeared to be unscathed.

On the floor were two green flower bulbs, or perhaps they were fruit. Split open, their contents oozed out and down into the gaps between the floorboards.

Tyrac charged the nearest guard, but his legs were uncharacteristically wobbly. He went down on his hands and knees only to have his arms rebel against him too. He couldn't feel his tongue, and the world around him was a blur. Before he went cheek down to the splintered floor, he had a glimpse of Leila right next to him, her face a mess of green goo. Her jaw was moving quickly as if she were chewing something. After she swallowed, she shoved something in his mouth.

Tyrac had just enough sensation left in his mouth to know that whatever it was, it was still alive.

"Eat it or die," she said. At least, he supposed it was something like that. There was a great ringing in his ears. He knew he'd heard the word *eat* for sure.

He bit down, once, then twice, and swallowed as best he could. It hurt, but it went down, writhing all the way.

Leila fell on him then. Her face awash with green slime and a mouth leaking a river of drool was the image he took with him as he slipped into unconsciousness.

IT WAS ALSO the image he awoke to.

As things gradually came into focus, he realized Leila was close, closer than she had ever been. She'd hugged him before, but this was altogether new. She was fully on top of him, her cheek squished against his. He deduced this because of the way she had to be positioned, not because he could actually feel her body. In fact, he couldn't see more of her because he couldn't get the muscles in his neck to turn his head.

He looked around as best he could by just moving his eyes.

They were on a flat stone surface at least a meter off the floor. The uneven rock wall he was facing curved enough that Tyrac figured the chamber they were in was circular, and they were in the center of it. Flickering light came from black candles resting in numerous misshapen alcoves carved into the wall. In addition, pale silver light came from another source high above.

Straining to see more of his surroundings, Tyrac managed to alter the angle of his head just enough to see that Grif was sitting on the ground, head resting against the wall, hands and legs bound with thick rope.

"Grif," Tyrac said. It came out more like *rrrriiiiffff*. Still, he was amazed that his tongue was working at all.

Grif's eyes flashed open. He shook his head as he stared at something Tyrac couldn't see.

Overlapping footsteps. Several people were approaching.

Tyrac felt Leila's eyes flutter open. He had recovered enough feeling in his face that he could feel strands of saliva sliding from the corner of her mouth and down into his.

Sweet little Ama appeared, flanked by two older boys. One of them was carrying a wooden bowl in each hand. The tiara on her head consisted of intricately woven stems decorated with black flower petals that glistened in the candlelight as if she had dipped them in water.

When Ama spoke, her words came much slower than they had earlier, and it was with an authority far beyond that of her age. She motioned to one of the boys. "Jol, the red sauce for the father and the hot spices for the mother. Gug, when the moon is in alignment with the altar, start the fire."

"Do we need to remove their clothes before we light the fire?" asked the boy who somebody had deemed worthy of the name Gug.

Ama clenched her fists. "What? No! That's disgusting."

"Your brother always has us undress our food. It tastes better without clothes. We can't eat the skin if they're wearing clothes when we cook them."

"My brother isn't here, and neither is my sister because these two hurt her. So I'm in charge of tonight's meal. The skin is the worst part, and it's not good for you. Besides, they're already strapped down. We're not untying them."

Gug bowed his head in defeat.

Jol, the other boy, took one bowl and dribbled its contents onto Tyrac's head, arms, and legs. The second bowl contained a powder that he sprinkled all over Leila's body.

"It doesn't make any sense to season her clothes," Gug protested.

"If you say one more word, tonight I'm going to make you eat all the leftover icky parts that nobody ever eats," Ama said. "Now get outside and watch the moon. If you don't remember what it looks like, it's the big bright circle in the sky."

"What about that one?" Jol asked, pointing at Grif. "Should I throw him on the altar too?"

Ama screwed up her face. "He's not ripe enough."

Jol peered at Grif. "I don't know, he looks older than Gug or I."

"Are you blind?" Grif said, his voice cracking. "I-I'm only thirteen!"

Jol shrugged.

"Grif, stay with us and eat," Ama said.

Grif shook his head. "I-I can't—"

"—eat your parents?" Ama finished for him, giggling. "It's easier than you know. You can think about it until we get back."

With that, Gug and Jol trudged out of sight, and Ama followed.

"She didn't even talk to us," Leila said when she could no longer hear their footsteps.

"Do you talk to your food?" Tyrac asked. "Grif, can you stand?"

"Don't you think I already tried that? My hands are tied to my feet and my feet are tied to a post in the ground. You got me into this, and you're going to have to get me out. I can't help."

"Leila?"

"I can't feel anything below my neck. I've been trying to move my arm, but they might as well have been amputated. You?"

"About the same," Tyrac said.

"At least our bodies are still drawing breath. Those were blight blossoms they threw at us. If we hadn't eaten the roaches, we'd already be dead."

"You put a roach in my mouth."

"You're welcome," Leila said, blowing out a breath that was warm against Tyrac's lips. "I didn't have time to grind it up into a powder and mix it into a bowl of honey for you. You can thank me for saving your life by returning the favor. How are we getting out of here?"

"Do you have your satchel on you?"

"Of course she doesn't," Grif said. "I can see it over there against the wall. Right next to some knives. I'm assuming they're yours. Your waterskin and your pack are there also."

"How many knives are there?" Tyrac asked.

"I don't know. I can see five, but there could be more underneath the satchel."

"Then pray that they missed my shiv."

"Where is it?" Leila asked.

"I'll tell you if you can move your arm before I can. Where's yours?"

"In my satchel."

"Grif, what about yours?" Tyrac asked.

"I—I'm not sure. They took it." He answered like a boy who knew what the punishment for losing a shiv was.

"How long before that Gug boy comes back and lights our fire?"

"We have until the moon is in alignment with the altar, whatever that means."

Grif said, "Who cares what it means? You need to get me out of here right now."

"Stop talking or you're the first person I'm coming to visit when I get my pouch of genital worms back," Leila said.

"You wouldn't," Grif said.

Tyrac said, "I'd believe her. She almost ate soup with people meat in it."

"You need to do something," Grif said.

Leila said, "There's nothing either of us can do if we can't move. The roaches aren't a perfect antidote to blight blossoms. It takes time." And there it was. It was faint, but it was there. Her voice had wavered at those last few words.

Leila exuded confidence and surety so often it was easy to forget those attributes weren't impenetrable shields against reality's cold, indifferent assault.

The three were quiet for several minutes.

"Leila," Tyrac whispered her name tenderly now that he had more control of his tongue. "I want to have our talk now." *While we still can.*

"No," Leila said, the waver in her voice had become a prominent oscillation. "This isn't over. We'll figure something out. The antidote will work. Just a few more minutes, and we'll be able to get out of here. Then you can say anything you want to me."

"I love you," Tyrac said. There, he'd just gone ahead and got it out. Sure, he'd said it to her before, but never in that tone.

"I love you too, Tyrac," Leila responded quickly, as if she was unsure of what she'd heard in his voice.

Grif was wide-eyed. The kid was going to hear everything.

"Hear me. I'm *in love* with you."

"What? What do you mean?"

"I've loved you for a long time. I want to declare it in front of the Hallowed. I want to take the vows with you."

It took her awhile to respond. "No. You can't do this to me. You're not supposed to—this isn't right."

"You're right. It's all wrong. It's not how I planned it."

"You planned this. You know the rules and you still … planned? Even if all this hadn't happened, you were going to tell me tonight."

"Yes."

Leila's tears began to land on Tyrac's cheek.

"You feel the same," Tyrac said. "I know you do."

"I do love you, like no one else, but you know I can't take vows with you."

"She's a priestess," Grif said. "She can't marry you."

Tyrac ignored him. "I had to tell you. It was eating at me."

"We're going to die, and you decide that it's still a good time to ask me to give up everything? To just let go of what I've obtained? To abandon my faith?"

"You can be married and still be dedicated to the Kin. We are all of the Kin. You don't have to give that up."

"But that's exactly what you are asking me to do. A priestess cannot take vows with anybody other than a priest. This is explicit in both the *Book of Kak* and the *Book of Viv*. Are you willing to do what it takes to advance in rank in the Kin?"

"To become a priest? Are you saying you would take the vows if I did?"

After more than a few seconds, Leila said, "Answer my question."

Tyrac could barely get the words out. "I can't."

"You mean you won't."

"I would if I could, but … no, you're right, I won't."

"I cannot be reduced in rank, and you won't advance. So, what you're asking me is impossible."

"I … I know."

"Then damn you for making me cry, Tyrac."

There was no good response for that. There was no taking the words back, and Tyrac didn't want to. It had been either seize the moment or risk not having a moment to seize.

Leila's tears continued to fall, and they didn't stop.

Not to be outdone, Grif put his head in his hands and began to produce tears of his own.

Tyrac closed his eyes and emptied his mind of all thoughts save for those of Leila. Time passed, and he took no notice of it. He focused on her and nothing else. The memory of her face framed by all that glorious, unbound hair, crowned in the orange of last month's setting sun. The smell of the soap in her hair mixed with the sweat on her skin and the ungodly stink of whatever noxious thing she had festering in her satchel when she had run up to hug him two weeks ago. The sound of her laughter when he'd smacked his forehead on a low-hanging tree branch the day before last. The taste of her tears as they ran onto his tongue. The feel of her body full against his, how she was soft and hard all at the same time. He meditated on these things, stored them deep, where they could bring him a measure of peace. In the end, when it came, he'd go there for comfort.

Wait.

The feel of her body ...

Tyrac heard approaching footsteps.

Grif started to wail.

"Leila, if I get us out of here, can I ask you again, some other time?"

After a moment, Leila whispered, "Yes."

"Good, because I can move my arm."

Leila strained to lift her head. Through a wall of spice-dusted hair, her eyes were puffy and red. "Get us out of here, and you can ask me anytime you want."

"I'll limit it to once a year. Now don't move." He could feel they were bound with rope both to each other and to the altar. There was a loop of rope around his wrist, but there was enough slack for him to move. He slid his hand between them.

"That tickles," Leila said. "I think."

His hand went down into his pants. There was enough sensation in his leg that he could feel his fingers probing for the shiv in its sheath on his inner thigh. He found it, extracted the small blade, and immediately sliced at the ropes he could reach. The ropes were thick, but loosely wound and secured by children. He made quick work of them.

Footsteps. Voices. All of them closer.

Reaching a hand around Leila's back to make sure she didn't fall off him, he found that he could move one leg to the side. He let it fall over the edge of the altar. He didn't know if he could stand, but he had to chance it. He rolled to the side and pushed up with his other arm. They clung to each other. Leila's face was in his chest, but he remained upright, and she didn't go down. He slid them both to a sitting position on the floor without damage by bracing one arm against the altar.

Everything tingled. Everything hurt.

It was wonderful.

"Kiss me," Leila said. "Do it now."

Tyrac was shocked, but he did it.

It was a horrible first kiss. They were sweaty and dirty. Tyrac's arm was bleeding and there was red sauce dripping down his forehead. The residue from the blight blossoms was everywhere, all over their faces, between their teeth, on their tongues. When Leila shoved her tongue in his mouth, sucking at him like she was trying to extract his saliva, he got a mouthful of the spices she'd been seasoned with.

Everything about it was disgusting.

It was everything it was supposed to be.

Leila pulled away, breathing deeply though her nose. She crawled over to her satchel where she extracted a small bowl, leaned down, and spat into it. Her dexterity increasing with each second, she dumped the contents of a small vial into the bowl with one hand and unlaced the tie on a pouch with the other. She shook the entire contents of the pouch into the bowl. The concoction started to bubble and hiss just as Gug and Jol arrived, each of them carrying lit torches.

"They're loose!" Gug shouted, as if stating the obvious was an accomplishment.

Jol turned and ran.

"You can't leave," Gug said. He was either the braver of the two, or he hadn't properly assessed the danger he was in, because he brandished his torch like a club.

Tyrac shoved his shiv back where it belonged, then collected his knives and managed to stand by leaning against the wall. With each movement, he was more in control of his body.

Leila was speaking fervent prayers to Kak and Viv while she traced symbols on the floor around where she'd set the bowl.

Gug didn't intervene when Tyrac cut Grif loose.

Leila made her way over on shaky legs, her satchel once again across her chest. Bowl in one hand. Her red, wriggling pouch in the other.

"Stay where you are," Gug said.

Tyrac moved faster than he thought he'd be able to and still stay on his feet. He blocked Gug's clumsy swing, grabbed his wrist holding the torch, and pushed. The torch fell to the ground. He swung Gug around, but lost his balance, sending the boy over toward Leila, who didn't fall when Gug rammed into her—primarily because Grif was gallantly cowering right behind her.

"You don't know how long I've waited to use these," she said as she forced the red pouch down Gug's trousers.

Gug launched himself at the floor, wailing in terror.

Tyrac retrieved his waterskin and his pack, then led them out and up the sloped entryway, only stopping to lose his balance twice. The rock walls ended and became branches that had been bound together and curved to form a short hallway.

They exited the base of the large rocks formation to find themselves facing what had to be the entire population of the settlement. Behind the crowd, a bonfire had been lit.

"That's more cannibal children than I've ever seen in one place before," Leila said.

"Hello, Ama," Tyrac said as the girl stepped forward, flanked by a line of guards, their pikes at the ready. Some of the children in the crowd had blight blossoms in their small hands. Others had torches.

"Grif has made his decision," Ama said. "He chose his father and mother over us. Once we recapture them, we will feed him until he ripens."

Behind Leila, Grif whimpered.

Tyrac raised his mask over his nose but left the hood down. "You know which way to run, right? Don't forget to take Grif with you. I'll catch up."

Tyrac's knives spun through the air, landing in the thighs of his intended targets, clearing them a small gap to one side. He pressed his attack, moving into melee distance, dispatching children with brutal strikes to necks, groins, and legs. He didn't kill anybody, but he broke noses and arms. When he snapped a kick at one attacker's knee, he knew the boy would never walk straight again.

Leila tried to pull Grif through the gap Tyrac had made, but a little boy with curly hair darted forward, jumped up and sank his teeth into her arm. She yelled, letting go of Grif.

Tyrac grabbed the boy by his throat and squeezed. The boy coughed and let go, permitting Tyrac to plant a fist in his gut to take the fight out of him. He shoved the boy to the ground.

The next second, he was forced to catch a blight blossom with one hand and sent it back where it came from. The young girl who had thrown it held up a palm to protect her head, but the bulb hit with such force that it exploded, showering her and the others beside her in the toxic green liquid.

Despite everything, Leila hadn't dropped her bowl, though the contents were angrier than ever, popping and smoking.

As Leila and Grif hurried ahead, Tyrac attempted to delay their attackers. It was impossible to dodge everything the crowd was throwing at them. A rock hit Tyrac's wrist, sending the knife in that hand disappearing into the night.

He spotted Ama in the middle of the throng and hurled his last throwing knife at her. The knife sailed true, embedding itself in her belly. She grasped at it, yelling for her guards. The guards and the rest of the crowd rushed to attend to her.

She probably wouldn't die.

Sticking a ten-year-old girl with a knife, even if she had tried to cook and eat you, was probably going to require an extra sacrifice to achieve atonement.

He turned to catch up with Leila and Grif but found that they were next to him. Leila had bent down to set her bowl on the ground.

"I made them some soup of my own," she said, grabbing Tyrac's hand and pulling. "It's going to be messy. We need to go fast. Don't look back, no matter what you hear."

Pushing Grif ahead of them, they fled.

Despite the number of children they had disabled, the roar behind them was louder than ever.

"They seem upset about something," Leila said

"They didn't get dinner," Tyrac said. "Also I put a knife in Ama's stomach."

In defiance of Leila's warning, Tyrac looked over his shoulder, just as the crowd reached Leila's bowl.

One of the children slowed long enough to kick it over. The moment the contents spilled onto the ground, hundreds of wiry red tendrils exploded into existence. The tendrils sprouted in all directions from a central bulging mass that pulsed violently as it grew. Screams filled the air as the tendrils wove throughout the crowd, entangling limbs, impaling flesh, twisting and turning until that part of the woods was an impassible, writhing discombobulation.

Tyrac believed in his heart that Leila's concoctions weren't magical; she created them using recipes contained in the Book of Viv. However, there were times when he wondered if there wasn't something else to them.

Tyrac squeezed Leila's hand. They were going to make it. They'd sneak back into Pallid. Grif would be a good little boy. Everybody would keep their secrets; life would get back to normal.

Except it couldn't. Not for Tyrac and Leila. Their world had been permanently shifted.

The three ran as long as they were able, which wasn't long, but was long enough.

When they stopped, and after they were satisfied that they were no longer being followed, they built a fire and rested. Leila extracted strips of cloth from her satchel to bandage the bite wounds that she and Tyrac now shared in common.

At some point, Leila pulled some indescribable mass from her satchel, took a bite, then offered it to the others. Tyrac declined, but Grif accepted.

"You two sleep if you can," Tyrac said after they had all eaten something. "I'll keep watch."

Grif didn't look like he was going to be sleeping anytime soon, but Leila rested her head against her satchel and closed her eyes.

Tyrac watched her. Her face relaxed and her breathing slowed. The memory of her lips against his was an intrusive thought that would not soon be banished.

Before she drifted off, he asked, "Did you really need my saliva? Is that what you were doing? I mean, for the ... whatever was in that bowl?"

Leila only smiled, which wasn't an answer, but it was close enough.

Ild's compulsion oftentimes made people reveal things they did not mean to, but Atli had never heard of a whole hidden city before. He shrugged. Fascinating, but what did he care? The knowledge got Ild no closer to his goal and was thus of no use to Atli either.

"Why does every asshole who ever fell in love think it makes them a goddamn hero?" Ild complained. "Siddown and wait for us to kill you, moron. Snow on fire, this is a really poor start, everyone. A really poor start. Who's next?"

The woman who stood next caught Atli's attention as sure as if she had thrown a hook in his eye. Darrish, scarred, and muscular, with a pair of crude hooks at the ends of her arms where her hands were meant to be.

But that was not what arrested his gaze.

This long-boned human woman wore wolf and bear fur, and a stole from which hung a series of glass birds. Pipers.

Inexplicably, she was dressed as a saltblood giant from the Troll Coast, the savage land of Atli's birth. Specifically the Vulg tribe.

How could this be possible?

Without preamble, the woman spoke, her voice flat, as though she understood fully the compulsion laid upon her and wished only to get it over with.

Atli sympathized.

"I am Gizella, of the Vulg. You do not deserve my story, but here it is anyway."

GIZELLA OF THE VULG
WILLIAM LJ GALAINI

The yurt was of typical size and make for a saltblood giant: a leather canopy with holes for light and ventilation supported by a central tree trunk. The trunk had been shaved down, and each family's yurt had their history delicately carved into the wood.

A notorious wrestling match won.

A joyous marriage consummated.

A grandchild taken by the frozen sea.

A clash with one of the other tribes.

Gizella, a lanky human girl on the cusp of womanhood, stood across from her adoptive mother, Old Cow, a salt-blood giant twice the height of any human.

Old Cow, the most imposing of the Vulg's matrons, sat with her back leaning against the yurt's trunk. A flock of glass pipers dangled from the high ceiling above, and their refracted light flitted across her stony skin. She was an elderly saltblood giant, deep into her second century, and the rougher edges of her hide had been worn down from decades of brittle northern winds, exposure, and warfare.

Today she appeared particularly grumpy, and Gizella knew this was finally the day that she would get Old Cow to concede. Her adoptive mother was going to yield. Frigid winds couldn't bend the crone, nor war hammers or ballista bolts. But a persistent teenage daughter was a far greater force than most could contend with.

Gizella had pressed Old Cow for weeks on the matter. The human teenager crossed her arms assertively, and despite her hands having been taken at a young age, Gizella still could cast an intimidating stance.

"I want to be among the smoothlings," Gizella stated. "I can't stay in this hut forever. I'm old enough; I can teach the Vulg what I remember of human language and in turn I can learn Vulg history."

Old Cow locked her eyes onto Gizella with authority. She didn't speak. She rarely had to. It wasn't because Old Cow was a ten-foot tall saltblood giant with stony skin polished down from decades of hard, Vulg life. What halted Gizella from continuing was that her mother never held a stern gaze at her human daughter, and yet here she was *angry*.

It was clear Gizella was finally getting through. Old Cow was only angry when afraid. The idea of Gizella interacting with smoothlings *scared* her.

"No," the giant crone said. "No, the smoothlings are too large and too foolish. They are as large as the largest humans at their age, and yet without wisdom. They will rough house with you and crush you. I won't have it."

Gizella pressed on. "What is my life, then? To be in this yurt as I enter womanhood?"

"Yes."

"Isolated? Alone? No future?"

Old Cow's shoulders heaved with a sigh. Seated on an auroch-skin cushion, the slumped giant's quartz-colored eyes met Gizella's dark ones at an even level. The giant was both beautiful and ugly all at once, with delicate glass beads woven into her coarse, ropey hair. Scars and nicks all over her stone hide told hundreds of violent and tragic tales, and her shale fingernails were worn down from work and worry.

All of that worry was now focused on her only remaining family: the tiny human Gizella.

"I don't trust them," Old Cow eventually said.

"Them?"

"Any of them." She waved her massive arm over Gizella's head to gesture through the walls of the yurt. "*All* of them. You killed the war chief. It only takes a moment for one foolish smoothling to get it into their head that they can kill *you*, and then they'll have bragging rights. Claim that they 'avenged' Chipped Horn."

While it was technically true that Gizella killed the war chief, she hadn't intended to. She had only been a toddler. Her father, the prominent merchant Methuzal, traded one of his redundant daughters to the notorious Vulg war chief Chipped Horn as payment for safe passage. In brutal flamboyance, Chipped Horn went to swallow Gizella whole as her father watched, but when the giant did so his throat bulged and his eyes watered until they burned wisps of smoke.

The war chief fell over, clutching at his neck as Gizella's feet kicked from within like a baby in the womb. Chipped Horn's mother, Old Cow, pulled the screaming toddler free of her cruel son's gullet. Gizella dangled by the leg, her hands crushed away by Chipped Horn's molars, as she dripped bloody sputum over the dead giant's face.

Old Cow's son, Chipped Horn, lay dead. She insisted this granted her the right to possess another child despite her age. It was the Vulg law of wartime adoption, and Vulg had never been out of wartime. This placed Gizella under the crone's care, and technically a member of the Vulg.

"Why would a smoothling ever want to avenge Chipped

Horn? He was a monster," Gizella countered. "The Vulg are happier without him."

Old Cow nodded in hesitant agreement. Her dead son was rarely a topic that ever came up, but Gizella long ago resolved to never hold back when speaking of his odiousness. He had pirated the seas, taken Gizella's hands, and shamed his mother.

"But Chipped Horn had allies and followers, still does, like One Eye," she cautioned. "They could influence the smoothlings—"

"Enough, Mama!" It was Gizella's turn to interrupt. She pointed a commanding stump at her mother. "I am a member of the Vulg, aren't I? By law?"

Old Cow's quartz eyes narrowed, but she gave a relinquishing nod.

"Then by law, I am a child of *all* Vulg. I require the education of the elder and the raising of the many mothers. I want to attend the wisdom yurt. To not give me these things would be neglect!"

With an angry huff, Old Cow nearly sprung to her feet. "Child!" she roared in frustration, rubbing her sore joints and settling back down. "You speak to your mother."

"I do! And I love you. And I know you'll outlast me in age, so you'll always be here to protect me. But I need to be part of the world." Gizella gestured to draw attention to where her hands would have been. "What other future do I have?"

Old Cow's resistant demeanor melted away. A look of shame cracked across her face as she gazed down at the pine needle flooring of their yurt.

"I am ... scared," the crone confessed.

Gizella climbed up her knee and lifted her mama's face to hers with her leather-bound stumps. "And I am *desperate*. I'm going crazy!" She laughed. "Besides, you'll be there. The many mothers are in the wisdom yurt during lessons. Maybe I can make friends? Maybe I can be accepted as more than something a saltblood can choke on?"

THE SMOOTHLINGS HAD their own dedicated yurt for daily lessons, activities, and training called the wisdom yurt. Given that their stone hides hadn't come in yet, smoothlings were particularly vulnerable to enemies of the Vulg as well as the Vulg themselves. Each smoothling was almost a hundred stone in weight and as tall as the tallest human, but they spoke more like children and processed things as emotionally and joyfully as any youth.

The many mothers of the tribe sat along the perimeter inside the yurt as each stitched leather, strung beads, or ground meal for their daily chores. Old Crow now sat among them, the oldest matron by far, and she pointedly focused on her tasks while avoiding the cautious, sideways glances of the other mothers.

Gizella sat, small and unobtrusive, at her mother's side.

None of the smoothlings had noticed their new student. They scuffled and laughed in the center of the yurt, each clad in lambskin for warmth since puberty hadn't heated their blood to the fiery levels of adulthood yet.

The elder saltblood ducked inside. Gizella had only seen him from a distance up until this point, but he was even older and more weathered up close. From his tattered stole dangled dozens of glass birds, each twisting the light into shafts of dazzling color. His artificer's optics were pushed up to his forehead, their kaleidoscope crystals jutting upward like grimy, uneven horns. With a satisfied nod, he evaluated his new generation of students as each smoothling fled to their individual rugs and sat quietly to await instructions.

He swiftly counted them and frowned.

"I was told there were nine smoothlings for me to ..." his

voice trailed off as his eyes landed on Old Cow in the shadows. Realization dawned on his face. "Oh no. No, not your *pet*."

It occurred to Gizella how difficult she had made her mother's life. Through her isolation, she had remained oblivious as to what Old Cow must have been suffering. Stigma might be only the beginning of her mother's ostracization, and now Gizella had elevated it into public humiliation.

She shrank from guilt, desperate to return to their yurt and never leave again. This was selfish.

But Old Cow nodded, as if expecting this, and stood slowly. Her breathing was stronger than normal, and it huffed the dangling hair in front of her face as she crossed the floor of the yurt. Smoothlings darted away from her footfalls as everyone in the yurt knew what was coming.

But even then, the elder simply watched the crone approach, a serene look upon his face. Gizella saw an almost pleased anticipation in his eyes as Old Cow's balled boulder of a fist hauled into his jaw.

Every attending mother and smoothling gasped.

A greenish, mossy tooth flew out of his slack mouth and smacked against the leather wall behind him. Searing blood on the tooth's root sizzled as it dripped down. He rubbed his cheek as he stamped out the budding fire from his burning blood. "I-I suppose I should thank you," he mumbled, nursing his wound. "That one was starting to rot. I'll blow a replacement."

As if to adjust his jaw back into place, he twisted his mouth about revealing two rows of mostly glass teeth.

Old Cow turned, her point made, and walked back to Gizella. With a snort, she sat and continued her craft as if nothing out of the ordinary had happened.

Every other mouth in the yurt was agape, except for the elder's. He seemed like a chore had just been accomplished. "Well, then. Let my ninth student come forward. Let's see her."

Gizella hesitantly stood, her rolled school rug over her shoulder, and walked to the center of the yurt. She had spent her entire childhood with only Old Cow's eyes on her, and now that an entire audience was judging the frail human without hands, Gizella regretted the entire enterprise. Being social was not worth this.

Aging and dying alone in Mama's yurt would truly have been better than this.

The elder nodded as he evaluated the tiny human before him. His aged eyes looked like the insides of dark river geodes. "Your name, daughter of Old Cow?"

"Gizella."

"Not a Vulg name. You still carry your human name, then?"

She hadn't considered that and didn't know how to respond.

The artificer nodded. "I am Ox. Just ... Ox. I've never had children of my own. I am the Vulg's master gaffer." He tapped his chest with a shale fingernail.

Then he pointed it at Gizella. "And you will be our first lesson. Tell me, smoothlings ... what do we know of humans?"

Several hands went up.

Ox pointed to a smoothling girl in the back. Her coarse hair sprung from her scalp and the nubs of womanhood were just emerging, but she was already tall enough to match the height of the largest human man.

She was elated to have been selected. "They can live anywhere!" Her lisp elicited giggles from several other students, but she soldiered on. "They can live in the desert or even in the cold like us."

Ox nodded encouragingly. "Correct, Boulder. Humans have higher tolerances to temperature. We *need* the cold to keep our blood cool. Humans have the ability to regulate their own body temperature, and they wear clothes and build shelters for—"

"Their blood doesn't burn?" a boy interrupted.

Ox fell silent, his head slowly turning to lock onto the rude student. The smoothling gulped and swiftly raised his hand in accordance with decorum.

With a gentle blink, Ox accepted the gesture. "No, it doesn't," he answered. "Humans bleed like the auroch, the walrus, and any bird."

More hands went up.

Gizella wondered how *she* was going to raise her "hand." Looking about, she searched for a spot to sit. A nearby smoothing boy pulled his rug aside to make room. He smiled at her briefly, his sitting posture placed his eyes at her standing level.

Ox continued to field questions from the class. Gizella hadn't seen another human since she was almost four, and given the elder giant's clear knowledge, she wondered what she would learn about her own people.

Perhaps she'd learn why her father gave her to a saltblood giant to eat.

As Gizella set up her rug next to the accommodating smoothling, another asked, "How do they do any of this without hands?"

The responding gasp from the other students and a few of the mothers took the inquiring smoothling by surprise. He looked about, bewildered at his apparent transgression.

Gently, Ox proceeded. "Humans have hands just as we do, but Gizella lost hers as a tiny child."

A girl snickered maliciously. "My mother says that Old Cow lost a son but gained a daughter."

The inside of the massive yurt fell silent. Nobody moved as worried eyes drifted toward Old Cow, but she appeared to be focused on her work and provided no reaction.

A wily look of mischief twinkled in Ox's geode eyes. "Well, Chipped Horn is the first and only Vulg chieftain to have been slain by a human. Even if it was by his own doing."

The boy that moved his rug looked at Gizella in awe.

MISPLACED

THE DAYS MARCHED FORWARD. Gizella sometimes fell lost in thought as she gazed at the glass pipers dangling from Ox's stole. As he continued to teach the class, the mothers passively looked on from the shadowy perimeter of the yurt, embedded in their own chores.

Somedays Ox would leave the mothers and take the class outside to walk around the extensive Vulg camp. Gizella positioned herself near the center of the smoothlings to keep warm from the frosty northern air, and it had the doubling benefit of making her appear less as an outsider and more as just another student. Even if her boots prints in the snow were half their size.

Ox showed the students the docks where the Vulg's pirate fleet was launched and maintained. Then he spent several sessions showing the students the ironworks in the middle of camp. And, finally, he led the class to his own hut for glassworks.

Glass pipers just like Ox's dangled from the thatch awning. He stood proudly before the small structure. It wasn't mighty like the ironworks. No hammers rang and no furnaces roared.

"This is my work. Glasswork. I'm the last artificer of my profession. Most smoothlings grow to serve the fleet and the war chief. One Eye calls for the efforts of everyone but me to control the seas." Ox tapped one of his glass teeth. "But glass is far more valuable than iron."

He paused for a moment, in thought. The smoothlings attention began to wander, but Gizella and the nice boy she sat next to, Brick, remained interested.

Ox eventually continued, "All of our land, all of Oldam's Temper, is a crater left by a furious god," he said, waving his long arm over the trees and the shore in the distance. "We had angered him, and he reached down with his bare fist and pounded the ground where we, the saltbloods, thrived. Oldham ended our civilization, and the age of humans began."

He reached down to his feet, brushed away the layer of fresh snow, and scraped up the frigid red sands underneath. "This dark sand is the pulverized remains of our people. Buildings. Temples. It carries the rage of a god in each grain."

Wriggling his fingers, he dramatically sifted the sand into the wind.

Gizella felt it wisp by her skin, several particulates catching in her hair.

Ox then drew attention to the stole around his neck. "See these glass pipers? These fine beads? We now use this sand for our glass." He made meaningful eye contact with Gizella and several of the smoothlings noticed.

"Beauty can come out of destruction," he said.

THE SMOOTHLINGS WERE ALMOST old enough to begin warfare training, so it was time for One Eye to come and evaluate the class. It was his right, as a chieftain during wartime, to claim whatever recruits he deemed fit for fighting.

And the Vulg had always remained at war.

Gizella stood on the end of the line, shoulder-to-shoulder, with her fellow classmates. Brick stood next to her.

"I'm scared," he whispered.

Gizella thought it ironic that he was the biggest boy in the class, and yet his favorite lessons had been about horticulture. He adored fungus, molds, and lichen. She'd even spied him petting the moss on trees.

She gently elbowed his thigh, being that her head only came above his waist. "I'll protect you," she said. At first she intended it as a joke to get him to smile, but when she caught him looking down at her, it was clear that he wanted it to be true.

Ox stepped in front of the student formation. "He can accept volunteers, as is his right. If you wish it, you may drop out of schooling and enter his training early. Some do, like he did and the war chief before. But you may also decline recruitment and finish schooling with the class. Afterward, he might still conscript you, but at least you'll have what I can teach as well as a vocation within the village as …" Ox struggled with his next word. He looked to the cluster of concerned mothers peeking out from within the school yurt. "Leverage."

Gizella couldn't tell if he was content with his word selection, but Ox again had mischief in his eye.

From the slagworks near the river, One Eye came. Around his neck rested a fresh necklace of human and troll ears. Flanking his sides followed his two meanest looking saltbloods, and over his shoulder he casually carried his stone-headed hammer. The head was once square, but it had been rounded over years of campaigning and piracy against anything and everything that the Vulg considered either a threat or an opportunity.

There was a danger to his movement, a malevolent eagerness. As he stomped closer, Gizella felt her chest jolt with each footfall. She looked to his scared mouth, an embedded fear rising in her chest. Feeling herself shrink from the sight of his size and posture, she remembered that Brick must be just as frightened.

She brushed her elbow against his leg again, to remind him that she was there.

One Eye approached, walking directly toward Ox. But as Ox opened his mouth to greet the warchief, One Eye stepped around him as if he were nothing but a tree in the way. Shrugging his hammer from his shoulder, One Eye rested the stone head on the ground and leaned on it.

"You're the new batch, then?" He took them in with his one good eye—the other covered with a steel sheet of metal bolted into his skull as a patch—before sighing with obvious disappointment. "Education, then. Hmmm. Education doesn't swing a hammer."

Gizella searched Ox for a reaction to One Eye's rudeness, but he gave none. He looked stoic in the morning light, rainbows springing from his glass birds.

One Eye continued, evaluating each smoothling closely, one at a time. "It is likely that I will call upon *all* of you. We launch two boats this coming season, not just one, and it will need a crew. Knowledge of our history carved into wood won't stop a ballista bolt to your chest." He paused at Boulder, squinting puzzlingly. "You're the funny speaker? That's fine. You won't need to talk when swinging a hammer."

She flushed with shame, her jaw tightening.

He moved on, eventually reaching Brick. One-Eye straightened his back to reach his full height. Only then, he could look down upon the fidgeting smoothling.

"Big!" One Eye declared with approval. "You're a big one. Want to volunteer? Get a head start? Hold rank before the others get pulled in?"

Brick froze, unable to look his war chief in the eye.

"Ox!" One Eye roared. "Did this one leave his spine in the yurt?"

The two bodyguards gave practiced chuckles.

But Ox walked around behind Brick and placed his hand on the smoothling's shoulder. "This one shows promise toward plants and roots. He'll be excellent for things we need like—"

"You know what we need, glass blower?" One Eye shot back. "Do you? We need him to know how to cauterize his wounds so his blood doesn't burn down the ship. We need him to know how to avoid troll poison, human spears, and rough seas."

The two giants glared at each other like titans, poor Brick doing his best not to quiver in between.

One Eye returned his attention to Brick. "Volunteer. Now.

Save yourself trouble. I won't have to conscript you later. Conscripts have it ... harder."

Gizella was relieved that she was still seemingly invisible to all parties involved, but she also said she was going to protect Brick. And so far only Ox had spoken against One Eye's bullying.

Gizella swallowed, cleared her throat, then spoke clearly and loudly. "Herbs and medicine," she began, "are things that preserve food and save lives far from home. Those are the things we need, and Brick is special for that."

Rearing back, One Eye looked down as if a cricket had spoken. Gizella's audacity at first seemed to anger him, but it melted into amusement.

"It speaks!" He looked back to his two companions to share his laughter. "And will you take his place? Swing the hammer against our endless foes?"

Gizella could think of a hundred retorts, but she knew that escalating the situation would only lead to making things worse. He was the war chief, and while the Vulg traditions of honoring an elder still held, they did so just barely. One Eye could flatten her with a hammer and suffer only minimal fallout among the mothers and elders.

In the end, he had the fighters and he had the boats. One Eye had the only means of the Vulg being prosperous.

She bit her lip, and waited until One Eye returned his attention to Ox for her to press her elbow against Brick once more. It was vital to her that Brick not feel alone.

"Brick? That's your name?" One Eye made a verbal note. "I'll make sure you are paired with a good breeder, if you volunteer. All of us on boats do that. Important to live on through offspring. But if you go digging into caves after mushrooms ... well, some may not find that mate-worthy."

The war chief gestured toward Boulder.

"Give it some thought," he said, hoisting his hammer back to his shoulder. Turning his back, he made some mocking gesticulation for his guards to laugh at, and the three returned to their loose formation and ambled back down the hill toward the slagworks.

Gizella's hair jostled from Ox's relieved exhalation.

Brick rubbed his eyes to hide his fearful tears.

Watching him from a distance, Gizella studied the war chief's gait; the sway of his hips, his fingers flexing on his hammer's handle, and his subtle limp favoring his right leg. He was a saltblood, as big as any.

But so was Chipped Horn.

GIZELLA RAISED her arm during a rest period in class. They had spent the majority of the afternoon rigorously discussing the history of the other saltblood clans, and she suspected that Ox did so in order to cleanse the morning's tension among the students.

They silently practiced their runes in small sandboxes at their individual carpets. As Gizella had already completed all of hers with her stump, she figured it was as good a time as any for her question.

Ox finally noticed her raised arm, and a look of worried hesitation crossed his face. She never asked questions.

"Yes, Gizella?"

Brick looked up from his sandbox.

Boulder continued to struggle with hers, her tongue flopped out.

A few other students looked over.

"How does someone become war chief?" she asked, doing her best to hide her malice.

A tiny smirk displaced the wrinkles of Ox's otherwise stern face, but he quickly suppressed it. "Sometimes a war chief is chosen before the prior war chief passes. Other times, the war chief is selected by the warrior party to take over the position. And on rare occasions—if there is an unresolvable dispute—a war chief can be challenged and defeated for his position."

The surrounding mothers had ceased their handcrafts to listen.

Each student had paused practicing their runes.

Brick sighed, drawing attention to himself as he gathered the words for his own question. "How did One Eye get to be war chief?"

Ox gave his typically encouraging nod, the one to foster classroom discussion. "Chipped Horn died without anyone expecting it, and since he had no sons, the position was open. Some wanted it, but One Eye had the majority of warriors behind him."

Boulder scoffed, her focus still on the runes. "Serves Chipped Horn right," she mumbled, her clumsy fingers trying to smooth out the rune in her sand.

A mother gasped from the crowd, alerting Boulder that she had been heard. For a moment the smoothling appeared terrified, but then her visage flashed to rage.

"What? He tried to eat Gizella. Gizella! Our friend!" She seethed, lisp sputtering, as her body heat rose and shifted the air around her.

Gizella's heart swelled with love. She had never expected someone to come to her defense other than Old Cow. And Boulder looked ready for a fight, ready to voraciously protect her.

Brick nodded in approval. "Did Chipped Horn eat humans before that?" he asked Ox.

Gizella looked back to Old Cow. Her head was down in shame.

Ox nodded in the affirmative.

"Does One Eye eat humans?" Brick pressed.

"No, no," Ox assured. "He does not. Those are old ways that brought Oldham's wrath."

"But he still murders all the humans he catches on the sea, yes?" Brick asked, eyebrow cocked.

With reluctance, Ox nodded.

"So the Vulg has so many enemies because we treat everyone like enemies?" another smoothling asked.

Other similar questions began flying among the students. The many mothers murmured among themselves. One mother declared, "The war chief creates the problems he is there to solve!"

Ox went to raise his hand, to ease the press of incoming queries, but he stopped himself. He allowed the roil of doubt.

Gizella once again looked back to Old Cow. She wanted to make certain she hadn't shamed or alarmed her mother. But the elderly giant sat quietly, listening intently, with dangerous eyes darting to and from.

The final question came. Boulder asked it, either out of naivety or fury, but it was finally put into words for all ears in the wisdom yurt to hear.

"Why do we even *need* a war chief?"

THAT NIGHT OLD Cow stayed near their yurt's entrance flap with a club in her hand. Gizella had to struggle with making dinner on her own, the utensils strapped to her forearms as she scraped at the iron cookware.

"Mama, why are you sitting there?" she asked from the fire.

Old Cow sighed. "One Eye will have heard about the uproar during learning by now. He won't dare hurt Ox, or any of the many mothers." She shot a worried look to Gizella. "But a human Vulg might not be a Vulg to him at all."

They ate in tense, attentive silence. The hours passed

without conversation, poems, or crafts as both souls held vigilance over their home.

But no one came, and eventually Old Cow fell asleep while sitting. Gizella dragged a woolen fleece over to her mother, draped it over her shoulder, and then took her own spot on the yurt's floor by the fire.

Next morning came, and Old Cow seemed tired, but relieved. One Eye never came, and the danger appeared to be clear.

"Perhaps none of the mothers said anything to him," she said, walking next to Gizella to the wisdom yurt. "Perhaps I give the mothers too little credit."

Everyone arrived and both the smoothlings and the mothers took their places for Ox's first lesson of the day, but the elder himself appeared to be running late.

Boulder took the opportunity to practice her runes in her sandbox. Gizella watched her struggle for a moment, then stepped over to encourage her. The one she was currently drawing was backwards, and Boulder noticed it just as she was finishing.

The yurt flap flew open.

Ox stumbled in, battered. Blood trickled from both corners of his mouth and dripped fire onto the glass birds woven into his stole.

Behind him, clasping him by the back of the neck, was One Eye. He brandished his warhammer at the smoothlings and mothers with a sweep of his free arm. "Tell me …" His snarl was that of grinding stones. "Tell me about what you 'learned' yesterday. Tell me *everything*."

Everyone froze.

Gizella looked to Ox, desperate to make eye contact. His elderly shoulders slumped at the sound of One Eye's demand. She wanted to rescue him, but he looked defeated and accepting of his fate. He opened his mouth to speak, a trickle of searing blood thickened by saliva dribbled free of his glass teeth. "I told them about the succession of—"

"Not you!" One Eye gave an angry shake to Ox. The glass birds in his stole, most now cracked with missing wings, tinkled sadly. "You. Tiny morsel." One Eye's hammer aimed at Gizella. "What is it you all learned yesterday?"

The other smoothlings instinctively backed away to their mothers except for Brick and Boulder.

This was it. This was the singular time Gizella had the attention of everyone and everything that mattered: the many mothers, Ox the elder, the war chief, and most of all the other students. The smoothlings.

Was Gizella going to prove herself an obedient Vulg by trying to mollify the raging pirate before her? Or was she a bold Vulg with a future?

"We learned that war chiefs only exist to fix the problems they create," she said loudly.

One Eye guffawed in amused shock at the audacity of the young human woman standing before him.

In the corner of Gizella's eye, she saw her mother stalking toward the yurt's entrance. She was slowly flanking One Eye and needed more time to get into position.

Gizella decided to continue provoking him to provide a distraction.

"We learned that the Vulg have wallowed in self-pity. Even a god couldn't kill us, and yet we just pirate the seas and live off the prosperity of other civilizations, like mites on crops!" She threw in the horticultural analogy for Brick.

One Eye's amusement faded. "You practiced your last words, I see." Kicking the back of Ox's leg, the elder giant buckled to his knees with a thump that shivered the yurt. One Eye shook with adrenaline. "You were never Vulg!"

He grasped his hammer with both hands, hoisting it high toward the leather ceiling. It came down almost faster than

Gizella could process. She didn't realize the saltbloods could be so *swift*. Rolling to the side, she dodged just in time. The impact quaked the ground with such force that both Boulder and Brick toppled onto their backs.

Furious at missing, One Eye bellowed, "Corruptor!" He raised his hammer again for another swing.

The many mothers pleaded for him to stop.

Brick coughed in an effort for air.

Boulder cried out in panic.

But Ox, despite having been beaten for the entire night prior, rolled backwards and drove his weight into One Eye's leg. It was like an avalanche rolling into a statue, and One Eye's hammer struck the ground aimlessly. The impact shuddered the yurt, shaking the glassworks in the ceiling and jolting the wooden pillar holding it all up.

The thick tree trunk supporting the yurt, with Vulg ancestry crafted into it, creaked in protest to the violence.

One Eye kicked Ox away, his stole flopping loose around his shoulders. Stepping on it, several birds crunched under One Eye's massive boot as he leveled his hammer low. He was aiming to swing along the ground, like he was reaping wheat. One Eye was berserk, now, and everyone's life was forfeit.

Gizella couldn't dodge such an attack in time, so she ran. Flailing her arms, she commanded Boulder and Brick to do the same.

His mass shifted, the hammer arcing through the air.

But mid-swing, Old Cow dove into him. Pounding and biting and grinding with her shale nails, she clawed at his remaining eye. His hammer flew from his grip, and it thumped through the air directly into the yurt's supporting trunk and buried itself into the wood.

A crack shot up the grain, splitting apart the etchings of Vulg culture and history. Splinters burst from it as the weight of the yurt, combined with the abuse of One Eye's temper, caused it to bend.

"It's going to give!" Ox yelled. "Out! Everyone get out!"

The mothers rushed the door, pushing the smoothlings with them, as One Eye and Old Cow continued brawling. The two collected forces collided, fighting duo versus stampeding crowd, tearing and tugging at the fabric and leather of the yurt. And finally, the dangling oil lamps above spun enough to spill.

Old Cow's gnashing and tearing at One Eye's one eye sent his smoking blood into the oil, and everything ignited. Panic, unleashed from the smothering smoke and flame, was now all there was to learn in the elder's yurt of wisdom.

Seeing the destruction spread, Old Cow shoved off of One Eye. But before she could reach out for Gizella, the throng of mothers and smoothlings carried her outside.

Blindly, One Eye swung his hammer after them. He was desperate to hit anything or anyone as the fire spread up the walls to the ceiling.

Gathering his senses, Ox coughed as he rose from the ground. Gizella ran to him, to support him and guide him outside. But One Eye heard the elder's wheezing and grappled at the two of them. The war chief's blind hands came down on Ox like clamps, pinning him down. Navigating the elder's frame, One Eye found Ox's throat and began pressing with all his weight.

"Die, old salt! I am the Vulg! Only me!"

Gizella shouted and kicked at the war chief, but her voice was drowned by the pillar finally buckling. Blasting apart in its center, the burning canopy drifted down toward them. The leaping light danced and bolted through the glass birds in Ox's stole. Gizella grasped one of the birds in her arms and rolled over One Eye, twirling the stole around her body as she did so. Then she darted under One Eye's chin, froth sprinkling her, and she cut back up over the wicked giant's shoulder and down his back.

Ox's marvelous stole was bound around One Eye's throat, the jagged glass birds all inward to his skin, and Gizella hurled her body to the floor to tighten the noose. All of her weight, heels dug in, pulled as the barrier of fire came down and ate all the breathable air. She couldn't see or hear or feel, but she held.

She held until Ox was released.

She held as One Eye clawed fruitlessly at his throat.

She held until the fire from above came down.

Perhaps there wasn't much future for an orphan without hands among the Vulg. But she would certainly make her mark. Gizella would be carved into the supports of the next wisdom yurt, Brick would tend to plants as he always wanted, and Old Cow would finally be proud of a child she raised.

The heat blasted. But before darkness swallowed her whole, hands found her. It felt like dozens of hands, smoothling and adult alike, and fire howled in her ears as snow was piled onto her, rubbing away the flames.

Two quartz eyes glowed before her. "Child?" Old Cow asked. "Child, are you with us? Please?"

Gizella opened her eyes. Her head was cradled in Ox's palm, the smoothlings gazed at her in awe in the morning light, and the many mothers stomped at the yurt's pyre to contain it. The shape of One Eye, a mound of still stony flesh, cooked in the middle of it.

Boulder looked to Ox. "What do we do now?"

Gizella's voice croaked back to life. She wanted to answer before anyone else did.

"Whatever we *want*."

Gizella sat back down. Though he knew Ild would not appreciate the unfathomable nature of Gizella's tale, Atli could not help but be impressed by it. Flabbergasted, really. He had faced saltbloods before, no troll counted the fiery giants as an ally, and the one time when Atli had been forced to battle a single giant warrior in a fair fight he had very nearly died. The thought that this human woman had not only killed one, but two, and not just a fighter, but a chief, beggared the imagination.

It would be such a shame to see her die.

A skinny boy in his middle teens dressed in a striped shirt and faded blue pants dragged a chair to the center of the room and stood upon it. A black frame held a pair of glass lenses in front of his eyes, making them appear larger than they were. He looked Andosh, though his strange clothing and oversized white shoes tied with bright white cloth cords placed him nowhere Atli knew.

In all, his appearance was subtly off-putting.

The boy spread his arms dramatically, and spoke, his voice cracking just a bit. "Harken, ye hoary hostiles, to the horrifying history I am here to herald." He turned to take in the entire common room, only tripping a bit as he did. "I am the dire draugh elf, Dhu! Destined to deliver dread decree on every dame and dude I determine." Dhu lowered one arm and pointed in a circle with the other. "My terrible tale takes root in just such a tolerable tavern as this, tippling a tumbler of..."

"I think I'm going to kill this one now." Ild's narrowed eyes glittered.

"Uh, okay." The boy pushed the frame up his nose, seating the lenses closer to his eyes. "So anyway, I was in a bar just like this one..."

WANDERING MONSTERS
JODY LYNN NYE

The ancient, iron-bound wooden door of the Genie's Lamp Inn screeched loudly on its hinges. Dhu looked up from his frothing mug of ale with a grumpy expression on his sable-skinned face. He lowered his white brows almost all the way to his sharp nose. Should one more of those human fools cross the bar's threshold, the drow swore he would not be answerable for his actions!

But, no. No Son of Adam was ever born to have such a bulky silhouette nor such massive wings on his back. Dhu recognized the chip out of the right side of the newcomer's head underneath the oversized ear and twisting horn.

"Chrysocolla, come close!" he called.

The gargoyle turned, his granite head grating on his thick stone neck as he moved. Gargoyles were the slowest moving creatures in the Known Realms, but they were fearsome, fearless fighters and faithful friends. The drow smiled. He could not help but think in alliteration. It was the way of all elven folk, dark and light.

Chrysocolla grabbed a polished oak stump as he passed the only other occupied table between the door and Dhu. He dropped it onto the flagstone floor with a crash and sat down. His big gray wings clattered around him like thunder.

"You look lost, my friend," Dhu said. He signed to the *ban sidhe* who served as barmaid to bring them beverages. "Why do you wander weary?"

"Clearing Sons of Adam and Daughters of Eve from Duke Haima's treasury," the gargoyle said. "All morning. Word must've spread that His Grace received the semi-annual collection of tax money. There had to be five dozen of the scum, all throughout the castle. They were busting down doors and kicking the guard orcs around. If it wasn't for me and Nok, they'd have cleared the strongroom."

"How fares the great gold dragon? Slumbers softly on his shifting silver?"

"Not great," Chrysocolla said, twisting his upper lip into a fearsome snarl. "It irks him when he loses some of the gold from his bed. It's fine when His Grace sends the Treasurer to negotiate with him when a withdrawal needs to be made. You have to trust the gremlins. They understand how dragons feel about money. Nok knows every coin he's ever slept on."

"Were you able to unseat the unscrupulous from their usurpation?"

"All but one," Chrysocolla said, with a rattling sigh. "Nok ate him. Or her. I didn't get a good sniff. Not my favorite meat, as you know."

"Aye." Dhu didn't like the taste of human, either, though he knew the rumors among them that claimed he and his kind did all manner of unworthy things. "Whither the others?"

"Ran away. They got some coin. Not much, but Nok is restless in case they try again."

"How is it humans have hunted here habitually?"

"Has to be since Ernesto the Explorer came through here a few years back," the gargoyle said, with a sigh.

As the sun rose toward noon outside the open door, drawing

shadows close to the feet of the statues in the town center, more of the Duke's subjects began to filter in. Dhu frowned and pulled his leather hood farther down over his face. He wasn't fond of crowds. One or two at a time, perhaps. At least he had his back to the wall. He sent a thread of protection into the whitewashed wooden panels. It bounded back at him with a smack to the wrist as if to say it was perfectly capable of taking care of him and all the others in this place.

The inn was a haven against persecution. Some creatures, having found it, never left it. Diamond, a small brownie who had been captured by humans in her home country, had escaped their toils near to the inn. In exchange for room and board from Esthelline, the establishment's owner, she kept the tavern spotless. Dhu shifted his mug, leaving a ring of moisture. It vanished as he looked at it. With a wicked grin, he moved it again, smearing further trace. It too evaporated. He could go on doing that all day, but he had no wish to fall afoul of the innkeeper. A mistress of mystery and mirage, she might afflict him with glamour that would cause him to drink from a spittoon or a chamber pot.

"Captain Chrysocolla!"

A trio of orange-skinned orcs dressed in chainmail with overtunics decorated in the Duke's livery staggered in. The leader had a filthy bandage tied over one eye. All of them were dusty and covered with mud and blood in equal measure. Dhu watched them with amusement. Before they had set a step past the threshold, a maelstrom of white energy rose about the three. When it cleared, their armor was polished to the last link, the bandage was as white as the moment it came off the weaver's loom, and all their garments were clean. The orcs batted irritably at the unseen brownie. They looked around, until their red-rimmed eyes set upon Chrysocolla.

"Captain!" the leader cried, rushing to the gargoyle's side. "We need your help!"

"What for?" the stone hulk asked, hoisting his pail of ale to his lips. "Can't a 'goyle get a drink around here in peace?" Two streams ran down his face past his earlobes. He lowered the half-empty beaker with a *thunk*. "Who's dead?"

"Agrippa," the second orc declared, his receding chin bobbing up and down with nervousness. Dhu felt shocked. Agrippa was his friend of many decades.

"Agrippa! He was supposed to join us for a drink here," Chrysocolla said, lowering his gray brows. "Curse all Sons of Adam and Daughters of Eve!"

The third orc gulped. "Only, he's not dead. Not yet. We think. Sons of Adam have invaded the library and are taking axes and torches to the Duke's books. He fled into a shelf of volumes, but it won't be long before they find him. Hurry! Orc Company Gar remained to try and drive them out, but they have a fell wizard with them. Lieutenant Futhark sent us to bring you back."

Dhu frowned. "What could he have that humans seek?"

"Didn't you hear?" Chrysocolla said, heaving himself to his feet. "Duke Haima inherited a bunch of rare volumes from his eldritch cousin, Duchess Lichebella. Humans invaded *her* realm, last year, probably looking for the Book of Return. It's in Haima's keeping, now."

"The tome to raise the dead?" Dhu scoffed. "The book's a myth."

"Not so!" a tiny voice piped up at his elbow. Quicker than lightning, Dhu snatched at the source of the sound, and dragged a handful of feather-soft cloth toward him. The fabric happened to contain the person of Diamond. The tiny brownie looked up at him with enormous, walnut-colored eyes. "I used to keep house for Duchess Lichebella. I saw her raise her great-grandfather, Baron Lichfield, from the dead. It was a terrible spell. Many creatures died in its making. The cleaning up I had to do!" Diamond shook her head at the memory.

"If those humans take the book, they never have to die," Chrysocolla said, taken aback. "I better get over there. Raise the alarm," he told the orc soldiers. "I want all the force at my back that I can get." Dhu sprang to his feet. He would defend his friend and the Duke, who had always been openhanded to the elves.

"I'll accompany you," the drow said. "The only thing worse than a human invading is having it come back again."

THE GREAT LICH CASTLE rose above Dhu with the comforting grandeur that can only come from crumbling stone battlements, tattered gray banners flapping in the breeze, rusty portcullises and grates over the cracked windows, and a general air of having been haunted for thousands of years. Dhu rarely slept indoors, but the one time he did stay within the keep as the Duke's guest, he had enjoyed the proliferation of spider webs, clusters of bats under every overhang, and rats the size of his childhood pet scuttling along the wainscoting. He'd slept as soundly as a svartalf.

The main entry was seldom used except for great funeral processions. Instead, Chrysocolla led his motley party around the rear to the kitchens, where the ghouls who tore apart animals for the Duke's feasts cowered in cupboards and underneath staircases, crying out their anger and fear.

Dhu kept one hand on the hilt of his dark-bladed sword. Hidden in his black leather jerkin and trousers, he had half a dozen dirks, and magic tingled in his fingertips. The brownie had armed herself with a mop. Chrysocolla needed no armaments beyond his natural attributes. His fingers were tipped with claws so fiercely sharp that he could climb the outside of the castle just by digging into the stone blocks. The orcs, now sixteen in number, huddled along behind them, looking about in fear lest the humans jump out of nowhere.

No torches burned in the sconces in the dusty passages, but Dhu was better off without artificial light. All the better for the element of surprise. If they could capture or scare off the humans, it would serve as a warning to future invaders.

Diamond held fast to the hem of his tunic. The others could see the dark glow his body gave off. It was invisible to humans and other creatures of the light.

"It's been a while since I've been to the Duke's library," Dhu whispered, feeling his breath freeze as soon as it left his body. The dank air was chill and smelled of stone and mildew. "Which way from the rear stairs?"

A *bang* sounded from somewhere below the stone floor.

"Just follow the sounds of mayhem," Chrysocolla growled.

The noises echoed hollowly in Dhu's ears until he found a sloping passage that led downward. Ghosts of past occupants of the keep flitted about his head, trailing long streamers of luminous silver ectoplasm over his face and shoulders. He batted at them in irritation.

"Get rid of them!" one specter wailed. "They disturbed my reading!"

Dhu felt the air warm as he reached the bottom of the passage. At the end of a broad hallway, red and yellow light flickered from a doorway on the right. Dhu tiptoed forward, light as a cloud on his feet, but there wasn't a hope in Hades that they could pass unnoticed, not with a great stone hulk like Chrysocolla on his heels. Or a bunch of fool orcs jangling in their ill-fitting armor. Nor yet with the brownie muttering about the mess. Dhu had to agree with her. Even in the dim light, his keen eyes picked out shattered doors and ruined furnishings scattered along the passage. One room still emitted smoke from what smelled like aged wood burning. Some of the Duke's favorite furniture had suffered from the intruders' attentions.

"Let me go!" a thin voice cried, somewhat incoherently, over the sound of crackling flames and the clash of metal on metal. "Leaf this plafe! The Duge will be fo angry!"

Dhu leaned against the door frame, from which the portal itself had been rudely wrenched, and peered inside.

"Oh, what a mess!" Diamond cried, her tiny hands flying to her cheeks.

A greater muddle could not have been made. The library, the drow's keen memory recalled, had been shelves upon shelves of scrolls, screeds, and sets of volumes bound in smooth snakeskin. Instead of a dragon, the Duke employed Agrippa, a well-read wight who knew every twist and turn of a plot, every page, and every pretty picture ever to grace parchment. Agrippa was a bit of a bore as a conversationalist, as a rule. Like the tomes he guarded, his discourse was dry and dusty.

He would have plenty to speak of now, providing he survived. Four beings in armor, all full human, tore at the carefully arranged shelves, seizing scrolls, pulling them open, then discarding them, either on the flagstone floor, or in the fire they had built in the center of the room for light. So many books had been destroyed!

Four more humans stood at bay, fending off attacks by the troop of orcs. Lieutenant Futhark slashed at the biggest fighter, a female wearing a chain hauberk that fell from her shoulders to her ankles and a polished silver helm over a gleaming silver coif. She countered his blow and twisted her blade to swipe at his knees. He jumped back, his heel going into the bonfire. He stomped in a circle to put out his blazing boot as two of his soldiers rushed in to face the female. Dhu counted the stripes of power on the human's breastplate.

"Fifteen," Chrysocolla said, at the same time as the drow concluded his calculation. "Curse it, that's probably Babylonia the Thorough. She's advanced since the last time she plowed through here. The Duke's got a price on her head. Wanted, dead or alive, for destruction and burglary."

"Let's claim that price!" one of the orcs at his back said, brandishing his stubby sword. "We outnumber the humans!"

"Not so swiftly," Dhu said, pointing. "The wizard still walks!"

Not only was the human spellcaster alive, he was prescient. The old man in long, dark blue robes turned toward the door, his eyes fixing directly through the veil of shadows that concealed Dhu. From the scrip at his side, he took a handful of enchanted stones and threw them across the floor at the drow.

Orange, gold, blue, and green, they tumbled, growing more dangerous with every turn as glowing white numbers bled into the air. Dhu leaped gracefully backward to avoid them, but one of the orcs was not as nimble. A blue stone struck the castle guard in the foot and exploded in a burst of azure light and the number seven. The rest impacted upon the wall of the corridor, covering it with burning numerals.

"Agggh!" the orc cried. He toppled sideways to the floor, writhing, clutching the stump of his leg. Dhu regarded him with impatience. Orcs had no stamina.

"Helf meef!" the muffled voice cried again.

"Agrippa, is that you?" Chrysocolla bellowed, leading the rest of the party over the threshold and into the fray. A human turned, swinging a hammer at him. He caught the metal ball on his upturned wrist and punched the fighter in the face with his other hand. The man went down, gasping, red blood spurting from his nose and lips. "Where are you?"

"Cryfocolla! Fave the boog!"

"Save the book?" The gargoyle looked around in bemusement at the shelves as he parried a sword blow with one sweep of his wing. "Which one?"

"I'll find it!" Diamond said. She bounded up into the shelves.

Behind her, the stacks of books stood upright and tried to sort themselves into some kind of order.

"Kill the monsters!" the wizard cried to the warriors. All but one of the humans turned away from the piles of scrolls, brandishing weapons. "We must find the book and spirit it away from here!"

Dhu strode forward and glared at him. "Me, you call a monster?"

"Yes, you, drow! Dark elf! Worshiper of demons!"

"True. But how does any of that make me a monster? We live our lives quietly in this locale, until you come charging, greedily grabbing that which does not belong to you!"

The wizard's eyes gleamed. "We have the right to take items of power away from evildoers!"

"Duke Haima is not evil," Chrysocolla shouted over his shoulder. Three more of the humans had joined the first one in the fray. Dhu could tell by the grinding of the big gray gargoyle's jaw that he was angry.

"It can speak!" one of the male warriors gasped, making the sign of the Eternal Circle. Dhu noticed that he had only two stripes on his breastplate. A newcomer to the ranks of the stupid and greedy. With near lightning speed, he threw his hand in the man's direction and knocked him down with a minor bolt of power. The cadet lay on his back with his mouth agape.

"You killed my shield brother!" bellowed a man with a bushy black brush of a beard. He yanked his axe from the skull of a fallen guard's.

"I only sent him to sleep," Dhu protested.

The wizard threw another handful of crystals bouncing toward him and his companions. These were all red. Should they touch the drow, they would burn his flesh like pitch. Dhu leaped up onto the nearest table, out of their fiery path. The company of orcs saw the tiny stones rolling toward them, and fled out into the corridor, screaming in panic.

"Come back, you idiots!" Chrysocolla shouted. The red crystals struck the walls and exploded in gouts of red flame. "Orcs!"

Dhu moaned to the gods. The guards had failed their fight against fear. It was left to him and the gargoyle to defend the Duke's demesne. He reached into his own belt pouch. Within, he carried only two handfuls of the square crystals of power. His abilities with the unseen arts were not as advanced as others of his kin. If he had known he would be facing a wizard of—a quick count revealed the awful truth—eighteen rings of power, he would have studied harder at the elbow of the eldritch enchanters. However, he had no choice. His aim had to be true! Chanting the spell of binding, he hurled the first golden group at the mage. The old man backed away but found himself against a rack that held the complete *Encyclopedia Mystica*, all two hundred volumes plus appendices. There was nowhere further to retreat.

"Aid me, Babylonia!" the wizard cried. The shieldmaiden shoved Lieutenant Futhark backward and dove into the path of the tumbling cubes before they could reach the wizard. They impacted upon her armor, but it was enough. Babylonia's body froze solid. She dropped like a dead weight.

The wizard's shaggy eyebrows flew up in alarm. He snatched the half-made lightning bolt out of the air and hurled it at Dhu. The drow scrambled for the remaining crystals in his pocket and tossed them into the path of the writhing web of blue light. Then he dove to the floor, his arms over his head to shield it. An explosion whipped white hot pellets of power against his back, burning like brands through the leather. He leaped up, angry at the points of pain that peppered his person.

No more magical resources remained to Dhu. The drow pulled his sword from its scabbard and glided toward the wizard. The enemy mage spread out his hands. Dhu saw the power build between his palms. Despite the danger, Dhu felt rage rise within him. Wizards and their ilk were weaklings and cowards, hiding behind their spells and charms. No more! He advanced, prepared to leap out of the spell's way.

"My Lord Balderol! I found it!"

They all turned at once toward the woman who called out. She stood on a heap of fallen tomes, brandishing a black-bound book almost as big as her body. When she opened the cover, the illuminated letter on the first page, the complicated red-and-gold knotwork drawing of a dog clutching its tail with its teeth, seemed to come to life.

"Helf meef!" the dog's face said, never letting go of its caudal appendage. "They muft not take thif boog!"

"Agrippa!" Chrysocolla shouted in relief. He held out a massive gray hand. "Gimme that book, Daughter of Eve!"

The woman, though wide-eyed with fear at the sight of the oncoming gargoyle, was nevertheless true of heart. Still holding the volume on her outstretched arm, she drew her sword with the other hand and began to back toward the open door to the corridor.

The other human warriors came to surround their companion. The wizard, though beginning to look weary, wore triumph like a cloak. He walked beside the warrior holding the mighty tome.

"Now, you will let us leave, or we will slay this creature," Lord Balderol said. His long hands continued to weave the spell he had begun. Fire danced between his hands. "You and your chaotic ways cannot defeat me now!"

Agrippa looked up at him with terrified eyes. Dhu hesitated. No matter how swiftly he could let fly his steel, one stab would sever the slender symbol. The wizard had the advantage. The drow looked around for anything that would aid him and his allies. Chrysocolla looked torn between leaping for the fighter with the book to wrench it from her hands and awareness of the danger to the librarian. The orcs had fled. The tiny brownie crouched upon a shelf, dithering with fear. The humans began to shift toward the broken doorway, with the wizard fondling his fell flame. It would wreak so much woe if it was loosed!

Dhu couldn't think. In the darkness of his cave home, or in the murk of the inn, his mind wasn't muddled. The drow were better in the cool blackness of night.

Night!

He called out to Diamond.

"There is too much light here. Extinguish all!"

The small female sprang up and spread her arms wide. It was the last thing that Dhu saw clearly.

In the next moment, the only illumination in the room was the blazing brand between the wizard's palms. Dhu grinned. The humans shouted and cast about for one another, but he and Chrysocolla had no trouble seeing them.

Magical flame was not like that fed by fodder. Should the spellcaster lose focus, the flame and the threat would die. He sped forward on feet too silent for any human to hear, moved around behind the mage, and put both hands under the old man's arms and dug his fingertips into the wizard's ribs.

Tickle, tickle, tickle!

"What are you doing? Stop it!" Lord Balderol shouted. "No! Hee hee hee! Ha ha ha!" The crackling fireball sputtered and disappeared. Dhu grinned in the dark. The wizard turned, flailing his arms to find his assailant, but Dhu was too quick for him. Every time Balderol moved, Dhu tickled him again. He kept the onslaught going until the wizard was on his knees.

As soon as the flames went out, Chrysocolla stormed forward, striking out right and left with fists and wings. The humans who had remained upright were soon on the floor among the masses of scattered scrolls and books, flailing for freedom. He piled them up in a heap and put his heavy hand down on the top body.

"All clear!"

"Oh, what a mess!" Diamond called in her tiny voice. "I can even see it in the dark!"

They sent her on the run to inform Duke Haima's gaoler. The satyr, a goat-foot named Obedion, arrived with a squad of turnkeys and fresh torches. Dhu blinked in the renewed light, but it was worth it. The wizard writhed helplessly on the floor, laughing until he wept. When a drow tickled someone, he *stayed* tickled.

As soon as the prisoners were removed, Agrippa loosed himself from the book, uncoiling into thirty ells of happy knotwork. He wound himself tightly several times around the shoulders of his three friends and squeezed mightily. Dhu and Chrysocolla gasped.

"I knew you would come to my aid!" Agrippa barked happily around his tail's end. "I owe you a debt, my dear, dear friendf! Drinkf are on meef!"

DHU SAT with his back to the stoutest beam in the bar. Diamond rested on the table by his right wrist, a tiny beaker clutched in both her hands. Chrysocolla hulked on his tree stump, and Obedion had his small hooves hooked into the rungs of a stool. Agrippa, his skinny body wrapped around the table and several of the nearby chairs, beamed as the ban sidhe barmaid poured beer for all of them.

"You are good foulf to have come to my aid!" he said, raising his mug in one of his many lithe twists. "Not only did you fave the Duke'f property, but my life!"

"We had to do it," Chrysocolla said. "Those humans think they can wander in and steal other people's property and still be thought of as on the good side of the balance? Hah!" He spat a mouthful of sand on the wooden floorboards. Diamond sniffed in annoyance. "And I had to leave my beer! That's grounds for punishment, if anything is."

"Hear, hear," said Dhu.

"Well, they'll do a stretch now," Obedion said, the horizontal slits of his pupils widening in amusement. "The Duke doesn't take kindly to trespassers."

Dhu lifted his stein to touch with the others, his teeth brilliant white in his ink-black face. "A toast, my friends. To those who are really on the side of right and rede, the real rescuers of the realm. To us!"

The story made no sense. Atli turned his head to one side, trying to square the irritating boy on the chair with the brave draugh elf—whatever that was—of the tale. But the compulsion allowed for no artifice. Was this boy some demon's trick, some disguise of the deadly dark draugh?

Fuck. Now he was doing it too.

"Is this a game to yoo, boy?" Atli growled the question between fanged teeth.

"Yes?" The boy appeared confused.

"What's your name, kid?" Ild asked. "Your real name."

"Lucas," the boy answered.

"And Lucas," Ild continued, "Is Dhu a real person?"

"No." Lucas's voice quavered as he spoke. "He's a monster in my Catacombs and Creatures game. He's me. I mean, I'm him. I'm the game master. But I did outsmart all my players, and it takes a real hero to do that. Not like all the other poseurs at the game store."

"Atli," Ild sounded tired, "please murder Lucas as slow as you can to show everyone this isn't a fucking game!" He turned to Atli and raised his arms as if to say, *You see the kind of shit I have to deal with?*

Axe in hand, Atli strode forward, only to find his way blocked by Masika, her slender sword raised.

"Touch him and the deal's off," the damnable woman said. "Everyone goes free."

"That wasn't the deal." Tiny teeth-gnashing noises came from Ild's card. "But fine. Let's get on with it. We can murder everybody in funny ways when this is over with."

Atli resheathed his axe over his shoulder, frustrated. Why was Ild playing along with this Masika? What did he know that Atli did not? The troll was not one for needless violence, despite his history and appearance, but he really had been looking forward to killing Lucas.

Later.

Lucas ran back into the crowd, leaving his chair behind. An even skinnier man dragged his table a few feet into the center space, creating a sense of tense drama as he prepared the space for his tale.

BETWEEN A ROCK AND A HARD PLACE

JESSICA RANEY

The rail-thin man sat down at the table, slamming his mug of ale, unconcerned that it spilled a bit. He was perhaps five and a half feet tall and so thin he might blow away in a healthy summer storm, but he made a lot of noise and puffed himself up and spread out his legs and elbows as if he could claim to be a much larger man, which was equal parts comical and annoying. He made a show of taking a big drink from his mug, and when he was finished, he uttered a satisfied "ahh" of refreshment followed by a long, loud belch. He smacked his lips and wiped his greasy, sparse mustache and goatee with his thumb and forefinger in an exaggerated motion of wisdom and thought.

"I'm Nobel Loya."

He looked around, as if he expected a shocked gasp of recognition from the crowd. When he didn't get any reaction at all, his big bug eyes bulged and his ratty face twitched.

"None of you know me? Why, I'm the most wanted man in Andos. They're looking for me from Norrick to Egren." He puffed out his chest and grinned. "But I'm slick as they come." He winked at the barmaid and wiggled his eyebrows. "I'll have had a fine lady, stolen the best horse, and be out of town before they even know they've been had."

Still, nobody looked impressed. Nobel reddened, took another drink, then sighed.

"These are fine tales if you're in the market for a sweet children's hour, but the one I have for you is a mite more exciting. I've been to every corner of this land from the Troll Coast to the Yellow Sea, and I've seen just about all there is to see. And I'll tell you what, I've seen some things that would make your blood run cold."

He motioned all around at the other patrons. "Word to the wise, if any of you is tender-hearted or weak-stomached, why, you might want to sit this one out. Maybe go have a nice warm milk with your mam."

When no one moved, he fidgeted and huffed a little, offended that his expert warning went unheeded or really, acknowledged.

"Well, don't say I didn't warn you."

THE SUNLIGHT TWINKLED through the shiny green leaves of the trees and a pleasant, warm breeze ruffled them, making the light appear to dance on every surface in the forest: tree bark, stones, and especially the clear water of the little brook that cut a merry path through the wood. There were just enough rocks and water to make the stream burble aloud, and the tall, dark-haired young woman who followed its path regard the noise as a soothing conversation.

The forest was a refuge to her and had been for as long as she could remember. A place far away from her mother, always yapping at her about her dwindling prospects of marriage. It was a haven from the vicious old hens in the village who gossiped non-stop about her. Magdalena spent every free moment she had amongst the trees and rocks. She studied plants and animals and, by the age of ten, knew the wood so well she could walk it in the dark of the moon and never be lost or afraid. She was an expert at finding medicinal plants and gathered useful bundles of herbs that she sold at the market. She saved all the coin she could; for what, she couldn't say, just that deep in her heart she had a wishful feeling and a churning need to get as far away from the Breadbasket as possible.

The little creatures didn't run from her. They regarded her as one of their own, and for her part, Magdalena acted as a steward to trees and creatures alike, caring for young saplings and helping any animal she found in need.

She hummed along in a sort of harmony to the singing of the brook as she looked for herbs for her medicine kit. A little bunny popped out from his warren amongst the tangled roots of an ancient oak. Its nose twitched and it hopped toward her with no hesitation. Magdalena smiled and knelt. She held out her hand and the bunny came close. He tilted his head contentedly as she scratched him behind his ear.

"Hello, Ed. How are you this morning?"

The little fellow squeaked and rubbed his face with his paw.

"Yes, it is a fine morning," she said, as if she were answering him back.

The rabbit rubbed against her hand again, asking for more scratches, and the girl laughed and smiled. She scratched him thoroughly behind both ears as she knew he liked. His soft, smooth fur was warm and luxurious to her touch. She enjoyed the gift of sensation he shared with her and hummed him a little song.

Magdalena and the bunny heard the noise at the same time. Something huge crashed its way through the underbrush toward them. She turned her head in the direction of the sounds, her brows knitted in concern. The rabbit dashed off to the safety of his burrow, leaving her alone to deal with the disturbance.

She smelled the creature before she saw it and wrinkled her nose as the pungent stink of a large dog filled the clearing. But the creature that emerged from the brush was unlike any dog she had ever seen. She was a tall girl, and the shoulders of the beast were even with her eyes. The creature's immense, square head was the size of a bear's, and its thick muscled jaws gnashed as it drooled. Its eyes glowed red, and it staggered around, the eyes not focusing on her at first. Then the thing's sensitive nose caught her scent, and it turned its head toward her and growled, so low and so deep that it made the ground around them vibrate.

She froze. Magdalena feared no creature in the forest, but this beast was not of the forest. Her grandmother had told her tales of such creatures, but she hadn't believed. She'd thought them only stories to scare her and her brothers into behaving. Not for one minute did she ever believe Matchi's Hounds were real, not until that minute of that day.

The great beast snarled and took a step toward her, its head lowered and its haunches tensed, full of energy as it prepared to spring at her. She held her breath but didn't close her eyes. Terrified as Magdalena was, she still didn't want to look away from the animal. So she waited to be torn apart, grateful at least her end would be memorable.

But the attack never came. When the hound stepped forward, it whimpered and crumpled to its knees. A long black arrow protruded from the animal's left side. The hound whimpered again and tried to lick at the wound, but it couldn't maneuver its massive square head around. It collapsed the rest of the way to the ground and panted in distress.

Seeing the animal in pain, Magdalena lost her fear and her instinct took over. She held out a hand and approached. As she did, she talked to it, softly.

"Easy ... I won't hurt you."

The beast bared its teeth and snarled. The girl stopped but kept her hand up and never broke eye contact.

"I know that hurts. I'd like to help. Will you let me?" She inched closer, her hand in range of the mighty jaws. One snap and it would be over for her, but she didn't think so. She had a feeling. She got just a bit closer. "Please let me try."

The hound growled. The growl began low and threatening but it ended in a high-pitched groan. He sniffed her fingers, whimpered, then licked them.

Magdalena let him for a minute, then she touched his head. "That's a good boy. Let's see if we can make it better." She petted him until he seemed used to her touch and more relaxed, then she examined the wound.

The hound was not of the forest, and neither was the arrow, she was sure of that. The shaft was as big around as her wrist and the wood ebony. The fletching was black feathers, and they glistened, iridescent and dark. If she listened close, she could hear the thing whispering in some arcane language. She didn't know the words, but she knew the meaning. Dark. Pain. No human made it, and no human shot it.

It was buried deep but had missed the heart. The skin around the wound pulsed and it looked as if it had tried to knit itself back together. When it did, the arrow sang its nasty song and the flesh opened up again, which caused the hound to cry out. If she could get the arrow out and dress the wound, she thought the hound would recover. But pulling a dark magic arrow from a mythical hound would not be an easy task. Still, she would try.

Magdalena gathered some moss and drew some clean water from the stream. She sat by the creature's head and stroked his slick black coat. "I know it hurts. I'm going to have to pull it out. I think you'll heal if I do. Do you understand?"

The hound pressed his head against her hand, then licked her fingers as if he understood. He lay flat on his right side, and his big red eyes looked into hers. The girl saw trust there, and she felt grateful. She patted him one last time, then stood up and moved to the arrow.

He yelped when she grasped it, but he didn't snap at her. She could barely grip it and when she did, an overwhelming taste of rot flooded her mouth and dark whispers filled her ears, telling her all kinds of terrible things and showing her awful pictures in her mind. She let go of the arrow and stepped back. She wanted to vomit and run from that arrow. It was what she should have done. She was only a girl. Evil arrows and magic hounds were not her business. Then she looked in the dog's eyes and again saw the trust. She spat the nasty taste out and willed the pictures and words away. Magdalena grabbed the arrow, put her foot against the hound's shoulder, and pulled.

The arrow screamed at her, and images of dying things in pain flooded her brain. She gritted her teeth and yanked the arrow free. She stumbled backward, still holding the arrow. She tried to drop it, but her hand wouldn't obey and release. Her palms burned against the glistening black shaft, and everywhere around her was the smell of burning, rotten things. More terrible dark images flashed in her mind, and the arrow screeched at her. The noise and the images held her, and she screamed as pain and fear coursed through every inch of her. Her heart and brain felt as if they were about to explode, and the arrow added a high-pitched laughter to the cacophony of horror that filled her ears. When she could take no more, a bright blue light flashed, blinding her. She dropped the arrow and collapsed on the ground.

Magdalena woke to the pleasant tinkling of the little brook and the chirping of birds in the forest. A huge pink tongue licked the side of her head. The big hound lay beside her, grinning.

A woman's voice, dusky, but with a musical quality filled the glade. "I can't decide if you're very brave or very stupid. I'm going to go with both."

The hound licked her face again and she patted him, then sat up. He sat beside her and leaned against her, as big dogs will do when they believe themselves to be little dogs.

The voice belonged to the most beautiful, yet terrible woman Magdalena had ever seen. She cut a dangerous and impressive figure in her hunting garb, all green leather and weapons. The leather glistened and shimmered, then changed as it adapted to the woman's surroundings, perfectly blending in. She leaned against a silver long bow and two silver knives hung at her waist. She appeared to be amused, but her face was as ever-changing as her armor, and it seemed to the girl that the woman could go from amused to ill-tempered quickly.

"You're Matchi, the Huntress," Magdalena said.

"See? Not all the way stupid. Just stupid enough to pull an arrow from my hound. I would have thought he would have eaten you, and I certainly would have thought that arrow would have driven you mad, yet here we are." The Huntress inclined her head to the girl, impressed. "What's your name?"

"It's Magdalena, Your Highness, or umm ... ma'am," Magdalena replied, unsure of how to address a goddess.

The Huntress ignored the breach of protocol. "Well, Magdalena, I'm in your debt. You helped my hound."

Magdalena blushed and looked down. "Oh, no ... ma'am, it wasn't a big deal. Anyone would have—"

"No, they wouldn't. Any other human would have tried to run away, and that hound would have chased them down and torn them to shreds, even with that black arrow in his side."

The hound panted and licked Magdalena's hand. He bumped her with his big head and leaned closer.

"And apparently he likes you, which is extra curious," the Huntress said.

Magdalena scooted around him to look at his side. The wound was tender, but it was nearly healed. She patted him on the head and ruffled his ears. "See? I knew you'd heal. Good boy."

"Please don't pet my hound. It's turning him into a pathetic lap dog." The Huntress barked a command, and the hound snapped to attention. He looked over at Magdalena one last time, licked her face with his giant tongue, then went to his mistress's side. "All right, so what will it be? What's your reward? I haven't got all day. Well, actually, I do, but I mean, I don't want to be here that long."

Magdalena scrunched her face in confusion. "I-I don't know. I didn't think of a reward. I just wanted to help him."

The Huntress rolled her eyes. "This amount of selfless kindness is sort of sickening. I cannot believe—"

Her words were cut off when a cloud of black smoke wafted into the glade. It formed up into a door, and a tall, gaunt man with a serious face emerged from it.

The Huntress rolled her eyes again. "You? What are you doing here?"

The man pointed a long finger at Magdalena but didn't say anything.

The Huntress huffed. "Is that theatricality necessary?" She looked down at Magdalena and gestured toward the man. "He's perfectly capable of speaking but he chooses his weird, long finger pointing for dramatic effect. As if harvesting souls isn't dramatic enough."

Magdalena's heart pounded faster. She felt a dread cold wash over her, and her instinct was to run. Her feet wouldn't move, and it wouldn't help anyway. She knew who the man was. He was Kohoc, the Harvester. There was no running from him.

"I should be asking you why you're here. This girl isn't yours to take," Kohoc said.

Magdalena jumped when he spoke and almost laughed at his high-pitched voice. Not what she expected from the Harvester. She had the good sense not to laugh, though, and the even better sense to shut up entirely and let the two gods deal with each other.

"Why this kid?" the Huntress asked.

The Harvester shrugged. "Why any of them? I don't ask why. I just take them."

"Ah yes, a real Mama's Boy. Does what he's told. Too bad for you, I suppose." The Huntress winked at Magdalena, and Magdalena paled at the casual way the Huntress regarded her and her impending death.

"As if you're any better? Running off to hunt down whoever angers her with your pack of mangy mongrels." The Harvester scoffed and motioned toward the hound.

"Hey. You take that back. My hounds are not mongrels, nor are they mangy." The hackles on the ridge of the hound's shoulders stood up, and he growled.

The Harvester pulled out a wicked, cobalt blue blade. Curved like a sickle, it glimmered in the sunlight. He pointed it at the hound. "Careful with him, sister. I only came for the girl, and I'm just doing my job."

The Huntress gave the hound a sharp command, and he stopped growling. "Let this one go a little longer. She helped my hound, and I sort of owe her. I promised her."

"That changes nothing, Matchi. You know that better than anyone. When her name comes to me, it comes to me. Her time is up."

"Who says it changes nothing? Just give her a little longer. She's a kid." She turned to Magdalena. "What do you want kid? Like a day? I don't know. Your human time doesn't always make sense to me."

"That's not very long," Magdalena said.

"Exactly," the Harvester said, nodding his head at Magdalena. "I can't give her more time. It's not mine to give, and it isn't yours either."

"Look, I can't go around in debt to humans, promising them things and then not delivering. I'll look bad. Well, worse. Anyway, come on. She's a good kid. Maybe kind of dumb, but brave and resilient. That arrow didn't scramble her brain."

"That's interesting. Another one," he said, obviously intrigued by the arrow. He shook off his curiosity and shook his head. "None of that matters. This is my work, Matchi. It's not pleasant but it's what I have to do, so please just let me get this over with, for all our sakes." He advanced toward Magdalena with his sickle.

Magdalena's stomach dropped but just like with the hound, she didn't close her eyes as Kohoc the Harvester came for her with his cobalt sickle. She looked him in the eye and accepted it.

Matchi stepped between them. "There has to be a deal we can make. Hey. How about this: we'll delay her harvest. She could be useful. You're always complaining about work. Maybe you need an assistant." She pointed to Magdalena.

"What are you even talking about?" he asked.

"As a favor to me, delay her harvest. Not forever. We'll put her into your service. She can take some of the burden off you. Delegate to her. She'll do that for … eh, I don't know, ten-thousand souls? Then you cut her head off and be done with her. She gets to live a while longer; you get a vacation once in a while." She looked to Magdalena. "Maybe that make him less of a bitc—"

"That's ridiculous. A vacation? Mother would never allow it." He shook his head, but Magdalena had seen something of a spark of hope flash across his jaundiced face. That scared her more than the sickle.

"She will. Hold on." The Huntress disappeared in a flash of blue light. She reappeared in another flash ten seconds later. "I spoke to her. She said yes, but only a thousand souls. Sorry, kid, best I could do." She shrugged apologetically to Magdalena.

"So, I just delegate a harvest to her? How is she going to do that? She's just a human."

"Yeah. That's tricky, huh?" Matchi thought for a moment, then she smiled. "I got it." She walked over to the hound. She bent down and stroked his head, lovingly, then she reached into his chest and pulled out his heart. She unsheathed one of her silver daggers and cut the organ in half. She shoved one half back into the hound. She pulled Magdalena's heart from her chest, cut it in half, then merged it with the hound's. She shoved it back in Magdalena's chest and fed the other half of Magdalena's heart to the hound.

The heart beat hot and thundered in her chest. Magdalena fell to her knees as she was overwhelmed with sensations. The sounds of the forest were magnified, every crackle of a tree limb or movement of a mouse roared in her ears. She sucked in a breath through her nose and smells she had never detected before were clear to her. She detected the scent trails of all the animals: deer, rabbits, foxes, and even the scent of humans, each one distinct in her mind. She looked up at Matchi, panting.

"What did you do to me?"

"Only made you immortal and self-healing. A little bit of gratitude?" The Huntress huffed.

"How does that help me?" Kohoc asked. "She can't harvest souls."

"Not yet. But she will." Matchi grabbed Magdalena's hand. With one swipe of her silver knife, she cut off Magdalena's right hand.

Magdalena's mouth hung open, and she was unable to even scream as she watched the blood spurt from her wrist.

Matchi grinned at her brother and ignored his squeaking protestations when she snatched his sickle from his hand. She took the cobalt weapon and held it to the bleeding stump. The flesh grew up around the sickle's handle, merging skin to steel.

Magdalena stared at her new appendage and screamed.

"Oh, relax, kid." Matchi looked to Kohoc and motioned to him. "Act like you're putting it away."

He rolled his eyes but pantomimed stowing the weapon. When he did, the sickle, now a part of Magdalena's arm, shrunk down into a cobalt blue hand. She flexed it. It didn't feel quite like a hand yet, but as the blue color faded to a lighter shade, she felt normal feeling return to her hand.

Matchi nodded approvingly. "See?" She winked at her brother. "Now act like you're going to take a soul."

When he did, Magdalena's hand glowed like the blue part of a flame and the hand turned back into the cobalt blue sickle. The pain seared her flesh and when the metal hardened it felt like every bone in her arm cracked. But the pain faded, and she waved the sickle around.

"There you go. Kohoc, you've got an assistant and Margret, or Magdalena, whatever your name is, you get to live a while longer." Matchi motioned to them, clearly pleased with herself. "You're welcome. Both of you."

"A thousand souls is going to take her a while." The Harvester eyed the girl. "And it's not a fun job. Besides, how do I know she can do it? Maybe it'll just be more work for me in the end if she screws up or refuses."

"If she refuses, you punish her." Matchi glowered at her hound, and he cowered, then rolled over and submitted to her. "If you train them correctly, they won't refuse."

"Humans aren't hounds." The Harvester stepped closer to Magdalena, almost protectively.

"No. Hounds are useful," Matchi said. "Well, she'll have to be punished if she refuses. Give her to Torment. She can take it. She held that arrow, and she'll heal."

"Yes, but what if she can't? Harvest, I mean."

Matchi scoffed. "Give her one to do right now and find out."

The Harvester sighed. "I suppose she's right." He leaned down and whispered a name in Magdalena's ear. "Fahd Tibbs"

As soon as she heard the name, a distinct scent flooded her nose. Fahd Tibbs. Her eyes burned and teared up. Magdalena closed them tight as cooling tears formed. When the pain receded, she blinked a few times to clear them. When she was able to focus them again, a red, luminescent trail appeared. Magdalena was overcome with the drive to follow the trail. She took off running through the forest, almost flying, her strides long and her feet barely touching the ground. She could think of nothing else but the name. Fahd Tibbs. She ran through the valley and up onto rocky ground. The terrain didn't bother her, and she didn't tire. She ran and followed the red trail.

Where it ended, a young man sat cross-legged on a flat rock watching over a flock of sheep. He was about her age, maybe a little older. He had dark curly hair, and his handsome clean-shaven face was tanned and glistening in the sunlight. He cocked his head when he saw her and wrinkled his brow in confusion. "How did you get all the way out here?" When he spoke, his voice echoed in her ears as if he were far away from her in a cave instead of sitting only a few feet away. The wind whipped up and Magdalena nearly drooled at the overwhelming scent of him. Fahd Tibbs.

She didn't want to do it. It had never come naturally to her and in fact, it was always the last thing she wanted. She didn't even eat meat. But the pain in her hand throbbed and burned, and the sickle formed and hardened. She screamed. She held her arm out away from her, shaking as she realized what she had to do.

"I know. It's hard." The Harvester appeared beside her. His face was sympathetic.

"He didn't do anything." Magdalena cried. "I know he didn't."

"No, he didn't. Hardly any of them have. But this is the job." He patted her shoulder kindly. "You do it anyway."

"I can't. I won't." Magdalena sobbed.

"Well then this happens," Matchi said. She raised her hand and closed her fist.

When she did, Magdalena screamed and fell to her knees. It was like holding the black arrow all over again. Light seared her eyes, unbearable noise rang in her ears, and her whole body convulsed with blinding, unbearable pain. Magdalena lost track of space and time. There was only agony. When it finally ended, she lay panting on the ground.

Matchi bent down and smiled at her. "That was like, maybe ten human seconds. Like I said, I don't exactly get your time, but I know it was short. Imagine that for much, much, much longer."

The Harvester helped Magdalena to her feet. "It has to be done, but you don't have to be cruel," he scowled toward Matchi. "You don't have to take pleasure in it. I never do."

Tears streamed down Magdalena's face. She walked over to the shepherd and cut off his head with the sickle. His head fell at her feet and his neck sizzled as the flesh cauterized. There was no blood, only the smell of seared flesh. Magdalena fell to her knees. Her metal hand glowed hot as if it had been shoved into the forming fires of a forge. She screamed and screamed and screamed until she was hoarse, then she collapsed to the ground.

When she woke up, her hand had returned to its human shape but remained blue tinted, and the young man's body lay at the bottom of the rocky outcrop as the sheep grazed and bleated around him. His head was attached, and it looked as if he had fallen and broken his neck.

"One down! Only nine hundred and ninety-nine more to go!" Matchi saluted them. Both Magdalena and the Harvester glared at her. She vanished in a blue flash.

"Is that what would have happened to me?" Magdalena asked, nodding at the shepherd.

"No, you would have probably drowned," Kohoc replied. He put a hand on her shoulder. "I'll give you three refusals. If you run into one you just can't do, touch this." He handed her a necklace with a smooth, round, black stone. "It has three charges. Use them wisely. It's the grace I wish I was allowed every once in a while."

"And if I refuse more than three?"

"Then Matchi will be delighted. It hurts you." He pointed to the body. "It doesn't hurt them."

"It's a kindness?" Magdalena asked, her voice bitter as she wiped the tears from her face.

"That's what I tell myself," Kohoc replied. "It will get easier for you."

Magdalena shook her head. "No. It won't."

Nobel Loya finished his tale. "And now she roams the country, lurking, waiting for her chance to take heads." He made an exaggerated slash at his neck and grinned at his audience. He gulped his ale. Taletelling was thirsty work.

At the bar, a tall, young, tan woman dressed simply in traveling clothes set her drink down, leaned her back against the bar, and smiled at Nobel.

"I've heard that tale before. You got some of it wrong though."

Nobel finished his drink and stroked his greasy mustache. "What's wrong about it, and who says so?"

The woman sighed. She held up a piece of parchment. It was a warrant for one Nobel Loya, sworn by a magistrate in Egren. "In between the heads, she also tracks down idiots for money."

Before Nobel could scramble away, she collared him and yanked him up from the tavern bench. "And one other thing," she held up her left hand. It was a faint blue color. "It was my left hand, not my right." She punched Nobel in the nose with a blue fist, "Let's go, idiot."

A loud twang reverberated in the tavern confines, and Nobel's head jerked backward and then forward onto a woman's shoulder who could only be the bounty hunter Magdalena from Nobel's story, given her dress and manner.

Following a straight line from Atli through Nobel's skull, a bloody arrow shivered in the far wall. Atli merely stood with his huge troll bow vibrating in his hand.

No one should have to put up with crap like that.

"Allz's wounds!" Masika leaped up, blade in hand, only to be stopped by Rainn's firm grip on her elbow. "Let go of me," she demanded. "He just killed that man. Right in front of us."

"I kinda feel like we should let that one go." Rainn's hold never wavered, despite Masika's wriggling. "That guy was an ass."

"That guy was my bounty." Magdalena brandished no weapons, but her tone commanded the space. Even Masika quieted. "You owe me for …" She stopped and looked around her. At the imp. At Atli. At Atli's bow, with another arrow waiting and drawn.

At the door.

"Bye, idiots."

As the door slammed behind her, Atli could not help a chuckle. Nobel had been the one compelled to tell Magdalena's story. She was not compelled to do anything.

So, she did not.

"Oh fuck." The quaver in Ild's voice brought Atli's gaze, and his bow, back up to the next person in the center of the room. Power shimmered the air between the woman's wiry frame as a burning village shed heat.

Atli had seen enough of those to know.

The woman, dressed in tight leather pants and a loose blousy shirt of blue-stained cotton, reached into a leather pouch around her neck and placed an object from it in the center of Nobel's table.

It was an eyeball.

The eye spun and glared at the people in the room, soundlessly threatening and surpassingly disturbing. At least Atli was pretty sure it was glaring. It was hard to tell without a face around it.

Sure was creepy as hell, anyway.

Before he acknowledged he had done so, Atli lowered his bow and relaxed the string. He glanced to Ild, who tried not to look as nervous as he obviously felt.

This woman was a sorceress.

She was not supposed to be here. Sorcerers were too big a fish for Ild's line: unpredictable and uncontrollable. The only thing to do now was to allow the situation to play out and hope for the best.

She focused on Ild. "You're a rune crafter's painting. I'm a sorceress. I can crack open mountains and you can be defeated with a candle flame. Does this seem like it was a good idea to you?"

"Say your piece and begone," the imp commanded. *Whatever else you might say about Ild, the little painting had balls of shining steel.*

"Very well," the sorceress intoned. On the table her disembodied eyeball rolled its gaze to the roof in frustration. "As I am trapped by your magic for the moment, I'll wile a little time as I figure out how to reverse your magic and tear you to confetti."

NOBODY'S THAT STUPID
JEN BAIR

"*Over a month spent tracking him down just to find him at the end of a rope.*" Hettie surveyed the mob of townsfolk surrounding the thief, who had managed to steal a great number of things, judging by their accusations.

"*Not surprising, when you think about it,*" Deryl said. Once a living man, he was cursed as a creepy, sentient eyeball who resided in a magic pouch around Hettie's neck. An accidental binding had resulted in a shared mental link that had taken some time to get used to. Having your every thought displayed before a highly opinionated man you'd never met resulted in a lot of threats on both ends until they'd worked out their differences.

"*True,*" Hettie said, "*but I was really hoping to find him fondling my artifact in a dark alley somewhere, so I could just bash him in the head and take it.*"

Deryl chuckled. "*If you found him fondling something in a dark alley, I doubt it would be your artifact.*"

Hettie poked at his pouch in chastisement, though she couldn't keep the smirk off her face.

They were outside the village of Cliffside, by a large tree with barren branches that stood at the base of a hill leading up to the clifftop.

The thief squawked as the hangman gave a test tug, cinching the rope tight around his skinny neck. "I have never stolen a thing in all my life," he insisted.

The hangman, a grizzled, portly old man in furs, cinched the rope tighter in response.

"I'm not a thief!" came the strangled protest.

"Liar!" came a shout from the crowd. "You stole my daughter's horse. What kind of bastard steals from a seven-year-old?"

"And you took my wife's necklace," said another.

"Sounds like he's been busy," Deryl said.

"He's going to be busy thrashing midair in a minute." Hettie considered her best course of action.

"That would be fun to see," Deryl said. *"Maybe we can hang him after we get the artifact."*

Another shout came from the crowd. "And me bag o' gold. It was all I had left for winter. Twelve silver, it was!"

"Did not," the thief insisted. He was lean and gangly, all elbows and knees, with dirty blonde hair hanging in his eyes. "Besides, it was only nine silver." Belatedly, he added, "And I didn't steal it."

Shouts of "Hang him!" rose from the townsfolk, the most notable of which was a hulking troll, ten feet tall with dusky green skin and bushy black hair that seemed to drape down his head like a waterfall, spilling into his beard and continuing down his neck until it disappeared under his clothes. His ram horns split into two points at the end.

Hettie circled the crowd, noting the lack of bows and other projectiles before giving Ouri the signal to keep an eye on her. The enormous lion hawk circled far overhead, his wingspan nearly as large as a troll's. Ouri was a fierce fighter.

Hettie came up behind the hangman, gripping his wrist. The

thief didn't weigh enough to break his own neck. One strong tug from the hangman might do it, though.

Startled, he scowled at Hettie, taking her measure.

Being Pavinn, she had golden skin and dark hair that hung to her waist. She wore her standard red vest over white shirt, black pants, and boots; though today she was sporting a feathered hat given to her by a couple in Arlea after she helped them out of a bind.

They likely wouldn't have been in the gift-giving mood had they known she was the First Daughter of the Deep Witch. Arlea and the Paradisal Islands had a long-running feud, but then, Hettie had left her island home long ago.

She tipped her head at the thief. "You can kill him tomorrow. I need him first."

"Who in Hagrim's name are you, woman?" the hangman demanded.

In a flat voice most people were smart enough not to argue with, she said, "Not important. He took something from me. I need it back. Kill him later."

The burly man grunted as the townsfolk listened in. "What'd he take?"

"An artifact. Nothing of value to anyone but me."

"Artifact?" the troll asked, his deep voice carrying. "Sounds witchy. You some kind of witch?"

She regarded him steadily until he broke eye contact.

"Not important," she repeated. "What *is* important is that I've been tracking this thief for a month, and I'm getting what I came for."

"I ain't no thief," the thief said, stubborn to the end.

"*You know,*" Deryl said, "*there's something odd about that troll. I can't quite put my finger on it, but he seems off.*"

"Besides being bigger, uglier, and dumber than the rest of this lot?"

The troll sniffed. "It's taken us more than a month to get

him strung up here. We ain't lettin' him go jus' cuz a witch says so."

"You're right, he is dumber than the rest of them," Deryl agreed.

The hangman spoke up. "Better head outta here, witch, afore you're strung up there next." Murmurs of agreement came from the crowd.

Deryl sighed. *"Never mind, they're all equally dumb."*

Hettie let a sly smile spread across her face. "Witch, am I?"

"You sure don't act like no normal woman," a man from the crowd called.

"Yep," said another. "Women around here know their place. You come strolling in here, bold as brass, meddling in our business. A stranger, for sure, and a witch ain't as much of a stretch as your neck'll do if we get a rope around it."

Hettie let out a soft chuckle, eying the group with a predatory gleam she'd spent her life perfecting.

A few of the wiser folk shifted to the back of the crowd.

"Why do people insist on learning the hard way?" Deryl muttered.

"So what? You think I can boil the blood in your veins and feed your still-beating hearts to your offspring?" She spoke slowly, letting the words sink in. "Curse your lands so nothing ever grows here again or have your chickens burst into feathers and guts?"

They stilled at her words and silence stretched across the open space like a graveyard at midnight.

Hettie reached for her magic, pulling tendrils of air from noses. "You think I can steal your breath?"

The startled oaths of those who felt her magic distracted the others long enough for her to reach into a pocket and pull out the whistle she carried. She used her magic to force air through it, creating a nearly inaudible high-pitched keen. Three short blasts had Ouri hurtling down from high overhead.

"Can I call the beasts of the earth and the sky to do my bidding?"

Ouri swooped low over the crowd, nearly clipping the troll. The lion hawk let out an ear-piercing shriek, voiding his bladder as he passed, leaving lumpy white streaks of excrement on heads before landing atop the rope over a branch.

The men's curses died down as they took in the enormous hawk, with her giant poof of golden feathers framing her face. Whispers of "lion hawk" went through the crowd. The birds were rare, but legendary.

Hettie kept her eyes on the crowd. "Surely you don't believe I can do all that. If you did, you wouldn't be nearly stupid enough to threaten me." Her smile grew. "I've seen a lot of things in my day, but I've never seen anybody *that* stupid."

Deryl snorted. *"Liar. Most people are exactly that stupid."*

Hettie ignored him, waiting for the crowd to respond.

After sharing nervous glances, they decided they had better things to do, watching her over their shoulders as they scurried back to their village huts.

Except the troll. He didn't scurry. Instead, he just looked disappointed as he followed the crowd.

In moments, only one man remained, and he looked content to stay. He had broad shoulders, red hair, and a strangely effeminate face. "You've sure got a way of making people listen," he said to Hettie.

Hettie loosed the rope.

"Thanks, lady," the thief said, prying the rope from around his neck. "I meant what I said. I ain't no thief."

She grunted. "Right. Where's my artifact? The one you *didn't* steal."

He swallowed hard. "Can you describe it?"

She sighed. "It's a stick about yea long," she said, holding her hands shoulder-width apart, "made of yellow rock."

His eyes lit up in recognition. "I know where that is."

Deryl chuckled. *"Of course he does."*

"But not because he stole it," Hettie thought dryly.

"Of course not. I'm sure it just fell into a bag he was carrying."

Hettie told the thief, "I suggest you fetch it."

He nodded eagerly. "I'm Teppe." He gave an odd little bow. "My friends call me Snag."

"Can't imagine why," she muttered.

He motioned for her to follow as he headed toward the village.

Hettie eyed the stranger, who stood nearby, placidly watching them. "Did he take something of yours?"

"You know, I spent half the day riling up the townsfolk. You sent them on their way in remarkably short order." He sounded more impressed than put out.

"Sorry to ruin your fun." She shrugged. "If you want, I'll help rile them back up, though there's easier ways to kill a man than to gather a mob."

He chuckled. "That there is."

Hettie waved Ouri off to do his own thing. If she needed him, she could always whistle.

She and the stranger headed off after Teppe.

"I'm Hettie. I didn't catch your name."

He shrugged. "I don't put much stock in names. Call me Plinth."

Teppe stopped at one of the first houses they came to on the outskirts of the village. It was a small, one-room hut full of items piled one atop another.

"Have a seat over there," he told them, pointing out a log in front of a fire pit by the side of his hut.

Hettie took a stance by the doorway. "I don't take chances with thieves."

Plinth leaned against the side of the hut nearby.

Teppe sighed but began rummaging around. "I don't steal. I came by this stuff as honestly as I know how."

"If you didn't steal all this stuff," she said, gesturing at the room, "then how did you come by it?"

"Remember how my friends call me Snag?" he asked, digging around inside a wooden chest. "It's because things kind of get caught on me."

Hettie snorted. "Some kid's horse 'snagged' on you?"

"Sort of," he explained. "She walked over when I passed their field, so I gave her a few pats and went on my way. By the time I got twenty minutes up the road, I realized she was following me. Must have jumped the fence. I didn't have time to take her all the way back, but I was thinking of what to do when the girl's dad rode up and accused me of stealing it."

She could see how that would look.

Deryl said, *"So he's got either really good luck or really bad luck. I'm going with good, since he's got a room full of stuff he never paid for."*

"He also had a neck full of rope, so I'd count it a mixed bag."

"True, but he didn't actually get hung. That makes you his good luck for today."

"I'm about to be his bad luck if he doesn't find my artifact in this mess."

Teppe continued searching while he talked. "That's how it started for me." He closed the trunk and moved to a small table, digging through a crate atop it. "Coins would fall out of someone's pocket and land on my shoe. The owner would hurry off so quickly I couldn't find them. A few times, I got the chance to give things back, but they just accused me of stealing. Nearly got hung for it twice, so I quit and just kept stuff."

"And my artifact?" she asked.

He turned in a circle, surveying the room. "Found it on the side of the road. Not sure where it got off to, though," he said with crinkled eyebrows. "I put it in a little sack. Red with black stripes."

Deryl said, *"That big troll had something like that sticking out of his pocket."*

"Really? Are you sure?"

"I'm sure. And it held something long and slender. Definitely the right shape for your artifact."

Hettie spoke up. "I saw a bag like that in the troll's pocket."

"Really? Borvan?" Teppe asked. "Are you sure?"

Hettie fought back irritation. "If Borvan's the troll, then yes."

"That's him," Teppe said, frowning. "Not sure what he'd want with it, though."

Plinth chuckled. "Thief against thief."

"I told you, I ain't a thief."

Hettie ignored him, turning to Plinth. "Why are you here?"

"Retribution. He took a woman's life."

Deryl let out a low whistle.

"Now hold on a minute," Teppe spluttered. "I ain't even a thief. I'm for sure not a killer."

Plinth locked eyes with Teppe. "I saw it with my own eyes."

"I ... didn't ..." he stammered. Swallowing hard, he said, "You're gonna kill me, aren't you?"

Plinth nodded, his gaze flicking to Hettie. "I can wait, though. No need to ruin anyone's day."

Deryl said, *"He doesn't think killing a man will ruin his day?"*

"Apparently not."

"Get me my artifact and I'll make sure you get a head start," Hettie said, stepping aside to let Teppe pass.

He came out, giving Plinth a wide berth. "Borvan lives on the far side of the village, but he's likely holed up at the Bloody Grin."

"Tavern?" Hettie asked.

He nodded.

"You seem to know a lot about this troll."

Teppe shrugged. "He's the only troll in the village. Everybody knows who he is."

"Fair enough. Lead the way. I could use a drink."

He scurried ahead with Plinth and Hettie following after.

"You promised him a head start," Plinth stated.

Hettie shrugged. "You seem capable."

"I'm capable of tracking him down, but my time is limited."

"Big plans?"

"More people to kill, probably," Deryl said. *"Not that it'll ruin anybody's day."*

The late afternoon sun drowned the village in long shadows.

"Not really, no. I've just got to get back to the rest of me."

"The rest of you." Hettie wondered at the odd phrase. "Like your family?"

He tipped his head. "Yes and no."

Deryl said, *"Is he trying to be mysterious?"*

"Not mysterious," Plinth assured them. "Just unsure of what I should say."

Deryl gasped. *"He* can *hear* me?"

Hettie froze mid-step, trying to think of everything she and Deryl had said since meeting the stranger.

Can he hear me? She scowled at Plinth, who had stopped too. *Can you hear me?*

Plinth blinked back at her. "I can hear your friend. If I wanted to, I could hear what you say back to him, but that feels like a violation, so I haven't listened in on your thoughts."

He resumed walking.

"Sure," Deryl said, *"when he listens to my thoughts, it's fine, but when he listens to yours, it's a violation. Where's the equality in that?"*

Hettie was too busy reminding her feet to move to answer him. Not many things caught her off guard. When she caught up, she said, "Who are you?"

He smiled. "Plinth."

"No, really."

"As I said, I don't put much stock in names. If I'm being completely honest, I don't really have one."

Teppe turned up ahead, and the pair followed a dozen paces back.

Deryl said, *"You're not human, are you?"*

At the same time, Hettie asked, "You don't have a name?"

Plinth chuckled. "I live in the Undergates. My memories in this form," he said, holding out his hands to indicate his body, "are limited."

Hettie's jaw dropped. "You're a demon."

"Never met one of those before," Deryl murmured.

"Not a demon," Plinth said, holding up a finger. "I know many demons, but I'm not like them. I'm … different."

What lives in the Undergates but isn't a demon? Hettie had heard stories of the Undergates, but stories weren't known for their accuracy.

"I'm afraid to guess," Deryl said.

Teppe ducked down a side street that echoed with talk and laughter. They stopped outside a wide building with a wooden sign covered in faded red paint. The words *Bloody Grin* were carved into it by what looked like slash marks from a knife.

Teppe looked apprehensive. "You sure it's a good idea to go—"

Hettie walked past him and entered the tavern, which looked to have the whole town jammed inside. A group of people were just getting up from a table near the door, so Hettie strolled over and took their booth before they noticed her.

Teppe followed quickly. No doubt deciding he was safer with Hettie than standing outside with Plinth, who was but a step behind.

It took a ten-count for the nudges of patrons to spread, but soon all eyes were on the trio, and their looks weren't kind. Mutters broke out in pockets, but Hettie stared down each group.

One man refused to look away. He headed over with a cocky look on his face, flanked by two of his friends.

Hettie waited until he stopped at their table, blocking the view of the rest of the room. When he opened his mouth, she blinked slowly, making her irises swirl like a tidal pool. It was a trick she'd learned from her mother. "You're not about to pick a fight you can't win, are you?"

The effect was instant. His already pale skin paled further, and he stumbled back as if he'd seen her burst into flame.

She turned away, dismissing him.

"Did you see ... She just ..."

He couldn't seem to finish his sentence, and his friends ushered him off to the far side of the room. With luck, the rest of the townsfolk would take note and let them be.

"I don't see Borvan," Teppe said, hunched in his seat with a very unconcerned Plinth blocking him in. "He'll probably be in at some point, but I don't think staying here's the best idea."

Hettie said, "So long as you don't take anybody's prized cow, we'll be fine."

He gave her an even look. "I'm never safer than when I'm snagging."

Plinth shook his head, surveying the room with an unnaturally calm nonchalance.

Hettie had been around a lot of tough men. If trouble was around, even the most confident man had a sense of alertness to them. Plinth didn't have that. He could have been watching a campfire flicker for all the concern he showed.

It bugged her not knowing what he was.

Plinth stood. "I'll get us some drinks."

"Whiskey," Hettie said.

Teppe perked up. "I'll take a—"

"Three whiskeys," Plinth said. He was gone before Teppe could finish.

Hettie asked, "How does this power you've got work, exactly?"

Teppe dug at a loose splinter of wood on the table, his skinny shoulders hunched. "It's not a power. At least, I don't think it is." He frowned. "It's not something I do. It's just something that happens to me. I don't even try most of the time."

"What happens if you do try?"

Teppe shrugged. "I get what I want."

Deryl chimed in, sounding fascinated, *"I wonder if there's a way to steal his power. That sounds incredibly useful."*

"What would I take with a power like that?"

"It wouldn't be for you. I could steal the belt off a man's trousers and watch him fall on his face with his britches down in the middle of town. That would be high entertainment," Deryl said, clearly delighted.

"You're incorrigible."

"I wonder if I could steal the shirt off a girl walking by," he mused.

"You're in my head, so you get to see me naked every time I change clothes. That's not good enough?"

Deryl sighed, *"How often do you ogle yourself while you're changing? I see what you see, remember?"*

He had a point. In the beginning, she went out of her way to avoid feeling violated by his presence, but he had no more choice in the matter than she did. Over the years, he had simply become part of her.

Namely, the part that never shut up.

She turned her attention back to Teppe, who was surveying the room. "You get what you want every time?"

He nodded.

Intrigued, she said, "Show me."

He blinked. "Here? Now?" He eyed the still-glaring people.

"Thought you said you were never safer than when you're snagging," she goaded.

"It's not the snagging I'm worried about. It's after that's the problem."

That fit with what he'd told her so far. "I'll deal with what comes." A room full of drunken villagers would be light work.

He slid out of the booth.

She had expected the crowd to react in some way, but

nobody did. She spotted a rugged man at the bar with a well-polished axe lying on the bar in front of him. It looked new. She gestured to it.

He looked at her like she was crazy, but he set his jaw and walked over to the man.

The axman scowled down at him, but just as he opened his mouth, a group burst into raucous laughter behind him. He spun. "What did you just say about my wife?" the axman snarled, his face twisted in rage.

Abruptly the laughter cut off, but one member of the group muttered something Hettie couldn't make out.

The axman shoved away from the bar to confront the man, his elbow knocking the long wooden ax handle, which spun around and came to rest in Teppe's hand.

With a shrug, he hefted the ax, going so far as to set it on his shoulder.

Hettie was amused to see that the entire crowd was focused on the axman and the heated argument at the nearby table.

"Incredible," Deryl muttered.

Drinks in hand, Plinth sidled up to Teppe, took the ax from him, and set it back on the bar before herding the gangly thief back to the booth.

"See?" Teppe said, reclaiming his seat. "Never safer."

Hettie grunted. "You should have tried stealing the rope they were gonna hang you with."

Teppe's look grew thoughtful, as if he was wondering if he'd been able to pull it off.

By the time they'd finished their drinks, the fight had died down, the axmen was back to drinking next to his ax, and the group he'd been arguing with had wisely decided to leave.

"Are we going to sit here all night?" Deryl asked.

Plinth said, "If the troll isn't here, where else would he be?"

Teppe thought for a moment. "At home, probably."

"We've got a better chance of finding him there," Hettie said.

"If he knows what he's got, he'll know I'm looking for it. I'd rather not give him time to leave town."

Placing a coin on the table, she stood to leave.

The nearby patrons watched them go. They hadn't made it three steps beyond the door when Deryl said, *"There's your troll. Ugh. I can smell him from here."*

Hettie spotted him heading their way. *"You don't have a nose."*

"I don't have a lot of things, but I've got plenty of imagination."

Borvan stopped when he spotted them, grinning to reveal yellow, broken teeth. "Didn't think you'd stick around," he said. "Who's the stupid one now?"

"Still you," Hettie said. Plinth stood next to her, his stance languid. Teppe slunk behind them.

Borvan's grin melted. "I ain't stupid, I'm strong, and I'll pound you into the ground if you don't watch your mouth."

"You prove my point. If you think muscle outstrips magic, you're dumber than I thought." A glance showed that his pockets were empty. "Where's my artifact, troll?"

Plinth spoke up. "He's not a troll."

"Are you blind?" Teppe squeaked from behind them. "Of course he's a troll."

Borvan let out a growl and stomped toward them. He smelled like rotting hay and sour apples. The stench of it was overwhelming in the narrow street.

Hettie circled to one side, drawing the danger away from her companions. She wasn't sure of either one's ability to fight.

Borvan was two steps away when she conjured a fireball and tossed it on the ground. Flames licked his boots. He hopped from one foot to the other, smacking at them with his hands.

While he was distracted, Teppe snuck forward, reaching a hand out. He never touched Borvan, but it didn't keep the troll's pelt from loosening.

It fell to the ground. Luckily for everyone present, his tunic was long enough to cover his thighs.

"*See!*" Deryl said, sounding like a child at a festival candy booth. "*It can be done.*"

Borvan spun around, glaring at Teppe. "Why, you little ..."

Teppe darted back behind Plinth.

Borvan lunged, hauling back to swing a meaty fist, ready to go through Plinth to get to his real target.

The blow landed, and Hettie heard the crunch of bone. But it was Borvan who screamed like a little girl, the pitch unnaturally high for a troll.

Plinth had a hand up, and blood was smeared on an invisible shield in front of him. When he dropped his hand, the blood fell to the floor.

"*Definitely a demon,*" Deryl muttered.

Plinth gave Deryl's pouch a chastising look. "Not a demon." He waved a hand and said words in a language Hettie had never heard before.

The troll seemed to ripple like a reflection in a lake.

"Hey! You can't do that," Borvan protested. Beneath the ripples, Hettie could make out another figure—a wiry man with mud-colored hair sticking up in all directions. The rippling abated and the troll image took the man's place once more.

"Illusionist," Hettie spat. She'd never met one she liked. More often than not, they were cocksure tricksters who preyed on unsuspecting folk.

Borvan's anger was replaced with indignation. He bent to pick up his pelt, revealing the hairiest green butt Hettie had ever seen.

All three of them turned away in disgust while Borvan tied his pelt around his illusioned waist.

"Don't know why you say 'Illusionist' like that. I'm not the one setting people's shoes on fire," he grumbled.

Teppe spoke up before Hettie could. "If you can make yourself look like anything you want, why would you choose to be so ugly?'

Borvan sniffed. "I'm not always ugly, but people like to pick on the little guy. They think twice about messing with a troll, though, don't they? All that bravery goes away real fast, then." He wore a cocky grin. "Bunch of chicken-hearted milksops."

"That's why you're always starting fights," Teppe accused. "You're not playing by the same rules as everyone else."

"That's rich, coming from you." Borvan laughed. "But yeah. I went from getting beat up every day to mastering illusion. I've had a lot of fun with my enemies over the years. A little bit of illusion goes a long way. Had one guy cut off his own friend's hand once. Best day ever."

"Quick, someone cry him a river," Deryl said dryly.

Any pity Hettie might have had for the picked-on kid this man once was evaporated. She fought back the urge to set him on fire again. "Where's my artifact."

He shrugged. "No idea what you're talking about."

"The red striped bag you had in your pocket earlier. I want what was in it."

"You sure it was in my pocket? Could have been an illusion."

His grin made Hettie close her hands into fists. She hated illusionists. "Nobody was looking for the bag earlier, so you had no reason to make an illusion of it. It was real."

His grin turned mocking. "Maybe it was, maybe it wasn't."

"This guy is just itching to die," Deryl said cheerfully.

Hettie reached out with her magic, turning the ground soft beneath Borvan's feet.

He yelped as he sunk a few inches, but before he could stumble out of the muck, it turned solid once more, holding him fast.

His troll image disappeared.

Plinth raised an eyebrow at Hettie. "How many spells can you do without words?"

"All of them," she replied with a shrug.

Deryl said, *"She had an unconventional education."*

Impressed, Plinth gave her a nod of appreciation.

Grunting, Borvan tried to free himself, but the hardened mud wouldn't give. He tried wriggling out of his boots, but had no luck there, either.

"Come on," Borvan complained. "I don't have your stupid artifact."

"Sucks for you," Teppe said, far braver with the troll trapped in place.

Hettie folded her arms. "I've got all night."

Borvan tried to get free again, lost his balance, and fell on his butt. Grumbling, he said, "Fine. It's at my house. I'll sell it to you for a good price."

Hettie snorted. "I'll pay the same price you did for it."

He squinted at her. "It's worth at least twelve gold."

That price was atrocious.

Deryl laughed. *"It's worth ten times that."*

"Sounds good. I'll pay it," Hettie said.

Borvan, Plinth, and Teppe all turned to her. "Really?" they said in unison.

"Sure. But I'll pay it to the real owner, not some sully-fingered, two-faced, ignorant, whiny braggart."

A sour expression met her insult. "For having such a poor opinion of thieves, you keep odd company," Borvan groused.

"I ain't no thief," Teppe said, unable to help himself.

Borvan barked out a laugh. "You're the thieven'est thief I ever saw. I've had a lot of fun with that fact. You've got the luck of the gods in everything but women. In that, you're almost worse than me."

"Women?" Teppe said. He looked confused until the expression cleared. "You talking about Mavery?"

"Of course, dimwit. What other women do you know? Did, anyway."

Teppe's lips drew into a line. "What do you know about Mavery?"

"I know you weren't the only man she kept company with. And I know she wasn't buying what you were selling."

A sour expression crossed Teppe's face. "She would have come around eventually, if she hadn't been done so wrong." He clenched his fists and scrunched his face.

Hettie wasn't sure if he wanted to throttle Borvan or burst into tears.

"I could have made her happy. Then she'd have only had eyes for me," he said, sniffling. "What woman wouldn't want all the riches a man like me could bring her? I'd have gotten her the moon if she'd asked."

Sucking his teeth, Borvan nodded. "You're right on that score." He glared off into the distance, lost in memory. "Some women only ever want baubles, along with a strong back and broad shoulders on her man. It's the trivial things that mattered to her. Not character. Or love. Or heart."

Plinth gasped, startling Hettie. "It was *you*," he said to Borvan. "You killed her. Then you left the house looking like Teppe."

Borvan jerked as if he'd been smacked.

"What?" Teppe asked, looking from Borvan to Plinth. "Are you talking about Mavery?" He got no response. "She was killed by a bandit who run her straight through with a sword. Everybody said so."

Plinth just shook his head in response.

"Mavery was a good girl," Teppe insisted. "It had to be bandits. Strangers, at least. Nobody who knew her would kill her."

"I thought it was you," Plinth said, meeting Teppe's eyes. "I saw it. I saw you leave her cabin with blood on your clothes, seething mad."

"Nobody saw anything," Borvan spat. He thought better of his proclamation and fell silent, though all eyes were on him.

"This entire town," Deryl said in wonder, "would hang themselves if you gave them enough rope."

"I saw it," Plinth repeated, conviction blazing in his eyes as he stared Borvan down.

Confused, Teppe said, "Wait. You saw him or me?"

"I saw *him*," Plinth clarified. "Only he looked like you."

"You killed my Mavery?" Teppe asked Borvan.

Borvan grimaced, then spat on the ground. "You show your true self to a woman and you expect them to be gentle with you. Not to laugh at you when you ask her to marry you. Duplicitous and fanciful, she said I was. Said she didn't even know me. Wasn't sure I knew myself. She could never marry me because I was a coward who hid behind *illusions* instead of facing the world and standing up for myself. She kept laughing until I showed her I could stand up for myself just fine. It was her that couldn't stand up for herself."

The hate and self-loathing on his face turned Hettie's stomach. She didn't know who Mavery was, but she hadn't deserved an ending like that.

"I-I-I loved her," Teppe stuttered.

Borvan yelled, "Your love was wasted on her! I did you a kindness!"

Plinth's voice was hard. "Killing her wasn't a kindness."

"Neither was looking like him while you did it," Hettie added. "Looks like Mavery was right. You're still hiding behind your disguises."

With a wave of the hand from Plinth, the troll image flickered and went out.

Enraged, Borvan punched at the ground, illusioning great cracks in the earth where his fists hit. Once he'd worn himself out, he looked up, his cheeks stained with tears, though his expression was full of rage. "Mavery deserved what she got."

Teppe screamed in wordless fury and barreled toward

Borvan, knocking him onto his back, though his feet were still stuck in the earth.

Hettie watched the two scrawny stick-men wail on each other.

"They're really pathetic," Deryl said. "Grown men and they can't even throw a proper punch."

"My money's on the ex-troll."

"There's enough fighting in this world," Plinth said tiredly.

Borvan pulled back his fist to throw a punch but smashed his elbow into the ground and hunched to one side. Teppe wailed on him.

"I don't get it," Hettie said. "If you saw the girl get killed, why didn't you take out the killer then?"

Deryl said, *"And miss all this fun?"*

Instead of answering, Plinth said, "Do you know how often demons fall in love with humans?"

"So you are a demon," Deryl said.

"No."

"Mavery was a demon?" Hettie asked.

A smile played on Plinth's lips. "No."

After a confused silence, he continued, "It's rare. What's even rarer is that a demon would give up his life to find her killer."

"So," Hettie reasoned, "The demon came to you."

"And you killed him," Deryl crowed, elated to finally get a statement right.

"No."

"Son of a fisherman's castrated pig fish," he cursed.

"The demon, as you call them, gave his life to give me the power to rise."

Hettie's eyes narrowed as she tried to piece it together. She still had no idea what Plinth was, but there were other pieces missing. "You've got his memories. It's how you 'saw' the killer."

Plinth nodded.

"Why didn't the demon kill him?"

"He went inside to check on the girl. She lived a few moments longer."

"And when he went after the killer," Hettie said, "he was nowhere to be found."

"Because he didn't look like Teppe anymore," Deryl surmised.

"Correct," Plinth said.

Deryl gave an annoyed huff.

A good shove from Borvan had Teppe toppling to one side, though his foot managed to land on Borvan's crotch.

Plinth made an intricate gesture with one hand and muttered a few words. A knife appeared near Teppe's hand, and he snatched at it, clambering atop Borvan.

Bent low over Borvan's head, Teppe tensed.

Borvan screamed in anguish.

When Teppe rose, Borvan curled on his side as best he could with his feet still trapped. His hands cradled one side of his face.

"How sporting of him," Deryl said, amused.

Upon Teppe's approach, Hettie said, "You didn't kill him."

Teppe was breathing hard, his face flushed from exertion. He'd wasted a lot of energy for doing so little damage.

"I've never killed anyone. I won't become a murderer on his account." He grinned. "Still, this felt good." He held up a bloody hand and opened it to reveal most of a severed ear.

Deryl snorted. *"He didn't even get the whole thing."*

Plinth put a hand on Teppe's shoulder. "Your honor is commendable."

With another mouthful of words in a strange language, the dagger flew out of Teppe's hand and back to Borvan, where it promptly plunged into his neck.

Teppe spun around, mouth agape.

Borvan gurgled for a few moments, then was silent.

"Your hands are clean," Plinth reassured him.

Teppe stared back at Borvan until Hettie gave him something to do. "Go find my artifact." She put her hands on his shoulders, nudging him off down the street away from the illusionist.

He stumbled away, staring down at the partial ear in his hands.

"My task is complete," Plinth said contentedly.

Facing him, Hettie saw that his outline was fuzzy.

"You don't look too good," Deryl remarked.

"It's my time to go home."

"To the Undergates," Hettie said. "With your demon friends."

He nodded, the motion making motes like sand fall from his face. He looked like a sandcastle falling apart.

"If you're not a demon, what are you?"

He seemed to find humor in her consternation. "I told you, I'm something else. But if I can't leave you with answers, I'll leave you with this."

Reaching up, he took her head in both hands, pulling her forward.

She had a dagger out and under his chin before their skin met, but he didn't try to kiss her. They had gotten along well enough so far, but no man took liberties without her say so.

Instead, he pressed his forehead to hers and a warm shiver ran through her, leaving her dazed and more relaxed than she'd ever been. Her limbs felt like jelly. She blinked, trying to get her bearings, and he waited before releasing her.

"What in the nine hells was that?" she muttered.

His smile grew. "A blessing of remembrance, should we ever meet again."

She gave her head a quick shake to clear it. Plinth was more loose Plinth-motes than he was solid body.

"I wish you well, Hettie Stormheart."

Suspicious, Deryl said, *"She never told you her last name."* But the rest of the motes seemed to fall all at once, leaving him talking to a pile of sand.

"Eat the angels," Hettie muttered in farewell.

They stood there staring at the multi-shaded sand for a long moment.

A gaggle of people spilled out of the bar, skirting her as they stumbled off down the alley, nearly tripping on Borvan. One of them let out an oath and kicked the prone body. When Borvan didn't move, the man bent over him in the dim light.

"He's got a knife in his neck."

Another man stood over the corpse while the rest of the group staggered on. "Who is that?" he asked the first man.

"I don't recognize him."

"Eh. Must be an outsider. Why are his legs stuck in the ground?"

"What am I, an oracle?"

The other man snorted. "If you was an oracle, you'd have known you were going to lose that hand of cards earlier."

The group at the end of the street hollered, "Come on, you two."

They went to join their friends just as Teppe approached from the direction he'd left in.

"I've got your stick," he said, hefting the red and black bag, open at the top to reveal a shaft of yellow stone. He passed it to her. "Where'd Plinth go?"

Hettie glanced down at the sand Teppe had kicked as he walked up. "He had to leave."

"Oh. Well, I probably ought to go, too, hadn't I?"

She nodded. "Unless you're keen on having another rope around your neck."

"I know. I ain't stupid." He cast one last look at Borvan's still form before slinking back the way he'd come.

"Teppe," she called after him.

He turned back.

"The next time something falls into your lap, drop it and leave."

"But then anybody could pick it up."

"Sure, but it'll be their neck in a noose instead of yours."

He shrugged, then kept walking.

Hettie shook her head. *"Think he'll listen?"*

"No," Deryl said. *"He is absolutely that stupid."*

Transport yourself home and go to sleep." Ild spoke quickly, as loud as a painted card could. "In the morning, you'll want to decide this was all a stupid dream, and it would be dumb to go chasing after an imaginary card in a dream-tavern!"

Hettie scowled at Ild, but twisted her hand into unnatural shapes as she whispered words of reality-wrenching magic. In front of her, the air puckered, bowed, and turned in on itself, revealing a tunnel full of wind and lightning.

With a final glare, the sorceress entered it and was gone.

"Thank the Anger." Frightened tension escaped Atli's body, and he replaced the arrow in his quiver. As he bent the bow against the floor to unstring it, he felt the heat of a terrible regard warm his face.

The eyeball remained in the middle of the table, its visage simmering anger of its own.

Atli sprinted the twenty feet to the table, his warrior's reflexes carrying him the distance before thought. His fist went up over his head and smashed down, shattering the solid wood and sending splinters flying in all directions.

Deryl the eyeball was already gone.

"I think we should move this along," Ild said, making shooing motions with his tiny hands. "No one wants to be here when that bitch gets her feet back under her. Who's next?"

A man in green-tinted plate armor, similar to the style worn by the Temple of the Sky but different in color and ornamentation, stepped forward, helm under one arm, and cleared his throat politely. Atli stepped back from the otherwise unassuming knight and returned to his place by the door.

He kept one hand ready to pull his axe, just in case Hettie should return early.

"Hello. My name is Sir Kendell." The knight waited for someone to acknowledge him.

"Hi, Kendell." Ild spun a finger in the air. "Kinda on a schedule now. Could we move this along?"

"I am happy to give my tale," Kendell said, "but if I might, may I make a suggestion?"

The weapons at Kendell's sides showed wear and use, but his armor gleamed, unscratched and new. Despite himself, Atli found his curiosity piqued.

"If yoo can make it quickly, yes?" The big troll frowned at Sir Kendell's open face. "Then yoo say your story."

"I was only wondering"—Sir Kendell paused and looked between Atli and Ild—"that is, I don't understand the quest we're competing for here. Going to something called the Undergates? Is it possible that we might find the task easier to accomplish if instead of just one of us being selected and the rest killed, we all could work together? In my experience sending one individual at a time when more are available is ..."

"Gonna stop you right there, hotshot." Runecrafted compulsion layered the timbre of the imp's voice. "Rules are rules. Spin the yarn."

In truth it was not a terrible idea, except that continued control of that many people over that great a distance would strain Ild to the breaking point. Their first attempt had left Atli caring for a seemingly dead card for weeks.

"Very well." The knight cleared his throat again. "Where I come from, mine is not an entirely uncommon tale."

SHORT STRAWS
KEVIN J. ANDERSON

Yes, a dragon was terrorizing the land, so the king had offered his daughter in marriage to any brave knight who slew the foul beast. Same old story. I was new to the band of warriors, but the others had heard it all before. This time, though, the logistics caused a problem.

"We could split a *cash* reward," said Oldahn, the battle-scarred old veteran who served as our leader. "But who gets the princess?"

The four of us sat around the fire, procrastinating. Though I was still wide-eyed to be part of the group—they had needed a new cook and errand runner—I'd already noticed that the adventurers liked to talk about peril a lot more than actually doing something about it. I was their apprentice, and I wanted for us to go out and fight, a team of mercenaries, warriors—but that didn't seem to be the way of going about it.

We knew where the dragon's lair was, having investigated every foul-smelling, bone-cluttered cave in the kingdom. But we still hadn't figured out what to do with the princess, assuming we succeeded in slaying the dragon. It didn't seem a practical sort of reward.

Reegas looked up with a half-cocked grin. "We could just take turns with her!"

Oldahn sighed. "One does not treat a princess the way you treat one of your hussies, Reegas."

Reegas scowled, scratching the stubble on his chin. "She's no different from Sarna at the inn, except I'll wager Sarna's better than your rustin' princess at all the important things!"

"She is the daughter of our sovereign, Reegas. Now show some respect."

"Yeah sure, she's sacred and pure ... Bloodrust, Oldahn, now you're sounding like *him*." Reegas shot a disgusted glance at Alsaf, the puritan.

Alsaf plainly took no offense at the insult. He rolled up the king's written decree, torn from the meeting post in the town square, and stuffed it under his belt, since he was the only one of us who could read. Alsaf methodically began polishing the end of his staff on the fabric of his black cloak. He preferred to fight with his staff and his faith in God, but he also kept a sword at hand in case both the others failed. Firelight splashed across the silver crucifix at his throat.

Reegas spat something unrecognizable into the dark forest behind him. Gray-bearded Oldahn chewed his meat slowly, swallowing even the fat and gristle without a word, mindful of worse rations he had lived through. He wore an elaborately studded leather jerkin that had protected him in scores of battles; his sword was notched but clean and free of rust.

I sat closest to the campfire, nursing a battered pot containing the last of the stew, letting my own meat cook long enough to resemble something edible. "Uh," I said, desperately wanting to show them I could be a useful member of their band. "Why don't we just draw straws to see who goes to kill the dragon?"

Alsaf, Oldahn, and Reegas all stared as if the newcomer wasn't supposed to come up with a feasible suggestion.

"Rustin' good idea, Kendell," Reegas said. Alsaf nodded.

Oldahn looked at all three of us. "Agreed, then. Luck of the draw."

I scrabbled over to my bedding and searched through it to find suitable lots. I still preferred to sleep on a pile of straw rather than the forest floor. The straw was prickly and infested with vermin, but it reminded me of the warm bed I had left behind when running away from my home. The straw was preferable to the cold, hard dirt—at least until I got hardened to the mercenary life.

I took four straws, broke one in half so that all could see, then handed them to Oldahn. The big veteran covered them in a scarred hand to hide the short straw and motioned for me to draw first.

Tentatively, I reached out, unable to decide whether I wanted the honor of battling the dragon. Sure, being wed to a princess would be nice, but I had barely begun my sword fighting lessons. And according to stories I had heard, dragons were vicious opponents. But I wanted to be a warrior instead of a shepherd's son, and a warrior faced whatever challenges they encountered.

I snatched a straw from Oldahn's grasp and could tell from the others' expressions even before I glanced downward that I had drawn a long one.

Alsaf came forward, holding his staff in his right hand as he reached out to Oldahn's fist. He paused for a long moment, then pulled a straw forth. His black cloak blocked my view, but he turned with a strangled expression on his face, looking as if his faith had deserted him. The short straw fell to the ground as he gripped his silver crucifix. "But, my faith … I must remain chaste! I cannot marry a princess."

Reegas clapped the puritan on the back. "I'm sure you can work something out."

Alsaf was pale as he shifted his weight to rest heavily on his staff. He nodded as if trying to convince himself. "Yes, my purpose is to destroy evil in all its manifestations. A divine hand has guided my selection, and I will serve His purpose." Alsaf's eyes glinted with a fanatical fury as he strode to the edge of the camp.

"Take care, and good luck," said Oldahn.

Alsaf whirled to face the three of us, holding his staff in a battle-ready stance. "I shall be protected by my unquenchable faith. My staff will send the demon back to the fires of Hell!" He looked at the skeptical expressions on our faces, then changed the tone of his voice. "I shall return."

"Is that a promise?" Reegas asked, and for once his sarcasm was weak.

"I give you my word." The puritan turned to stride into the deep stillness of the forest night, crunching through the underbrush.

It was the only promise Alsaf ever broke.

"For our honor, we must continue." Oldahn held three straws in his hand, thrusting them forward. "Come, Reegas. Draw first."

Reegas cursed under his breath and reached out to grab a straw without even pausing for thought. A broad grin split his face. He held a long straw.

I came forward, looking intently at the two straws, two chances. One would pit me against a scaly, fire-breathing demon and the other would give me a reprieve. Knowing that the dragon had already defeated one warrior, I decided the princess wasn't so desirable after all. Alsaf had seemed so strong, so confident, so determined. I hesitated, hoping the puritan would return at the last possible moment.

But he didn't, and I picked a straw. It was long.

Oldahn stared at the short straw remaining in his hand. Cold battle-lust boiled in his eyes. "Very well, I have a dragon to slay, a death to avenge, and a princess to win. I had thought it too late in my life to settle down in marriage, but I will adapt. My brave exploits should be sung by minstrels all across the kingdom."

"Our kingdom doesn't have any minstrels, Oldahn," I pointed out.

The old warrior sighed. "I should have volunteered to go first anyway. I am the leader of our band."

"Our band?" Reegas said, sulking in his crusty old chainmail shirt. "Rust, Oldahn, with you gone we aren't much of a band anymore."

Oldahn patted his heavy broadsword and walked stiffly across the camp. It was a beautiful day, and the sun broke through in scattered patches of green light. Oldahn looked around as if for one last time. He turned to walk away, calling back to us just before he vanished into the tangled distance, "Don't be so sure I won't be coming back."

By nightfall, we were sure.

The campfire was lonely with only Reegas and me sitting by it. Oldahn had fallen, and the fact that he was the best warrior in our group (old mercenaries are, by definition, good warriors) didn't improve our confidence. I could hardly believe the great fighter I had revered so much had been *slain*. It wasn't supposed to be this way.

I looked at Reegas, fidgeting in his battered chainmail. "Well, Reegas, do you want to wait until morning, or draw straws now?"

"Rust! Let's get it over with," he said. His eyes were bloodshot. "This better be one hell of a princess."

I picked up two straws, one long, the other short. I held them out to Reegas, and he spat into the fire before looking at me. I masked my expression with some effort. Reegas reached forward and pulled the short straw.

"Bloodrust and battlerot!" he howled, jerking at the ends of the straw as if trying to stretch it longer. He crumpled it in his grip and threw it into the fire, then sank into a squat by my cookpots. "Aww, Kendell—now I can't teach you some things! I meant to take you over to the inn one night where you would ..."

I looked at him with a half-smile, raising an eyebrow. "Reegas, do you think Sarna takes no other customers besides yourself?"

Wonder and shock lit up his craggy face. "You? Rust!" Reegas laughed loudly, a nervous blustering laugh. He clapped me on the back with perverse pride. "I won't feel sorry for you anymore, Kendell." He drew his sword and leaped into the air, slashing at a branch overhead. "But I'm gonna get that rustin' princess for myself. Maybe royalty knows a few tricks the common hussies don't."

He turned with a new excitement, dancing out of camp, waving farewell.

Alone by the campfire, I waited the long hours as the dusk collapsed into darkness. The forest filled with the noisy silence of a wild night. As the stars began to shine, I lay on the cold ground with my head propped against the rough bark of an old oak. I gave up sleeping on straw in fear that I would have dreams of dark scales and death.

The branches above me looked like the black framework of a broken lattice supporting the stars. The mockingly pleasant fire and the empty campsite made me feel intensely lonely; and for the first time I felt the true pain of my friends' losses. I had wanted to be one of them and now they were all gone.

I remembered some of the stories they had told me, but I hadn't quite fit in with the rest of the band yet. I was a novice; I hadn't yet fought battles with them, hadn't helped them in any way. And now Alsaf and Oldahn were gone, and Reegas had a good chance of joining them.

Since I had talked my way into accompanying the band, nothing much had happened. Until the dragon came, that is.

Of course, if I had known my first adventure might involve a battle with a large reptilian terror, I might have put up with my dull old life a little longer. My father was a shepherd, spending so much time out with his flocks that he had begun to look like one of his sheep. Imagine watching thirty animals eat grass hour after hour! My mother was a weaver, spending every day hunched over her loom, hurling her shuttle back and forth, watching the threads line themselves up one at a time. She even walked with a jerky back and forth motion, as if bouncing to the beat of a flying shuttle.

Me, I'd just as soon be out fighting bandits, dispatching troublesome wolves, or chasing the odd sorcerer away under the grave risk of having an indelible curse hurled at me. That's excitement—but slaying a dragon is going a bit too far!

I couldn't sleep and lay waiting, listening to the night sounds. At every rustle of leaves I jumped, peering into the shadows, hoping it might be Reegas returning or Oldahn or even Alsaf.

But no one came.

Finally, at dawn, I threw the last long straw on the dirt and ground it under my heel. I had only ever used my sword to cut up meat for the cook fires. I was alone. No one watched me, or pressured me, or insisted that I too go out and challenge the dragon. I could have just crept back home, helped my father tend sheep, helped my mother with her weaving. But somehow that kind of life seemed worse than facing a dragon.

I stared at the blade of my sword, thinking of my comrades. Alsaf and Oldahn and Reegas had been my friends, and I was the only one who could avenge them. Only I remained of the entire mercenary band. I had been with Oldahn long enough, heard his tales of glory, seen how the group worked together as a team. I couldn't just let the dragon have its victory.

Muttering a few curses I had picked up from Reegas, I left the dead campfire behind and set off through the forest.

The forest floor was impervious to the sunshine that dribbled through the woven leaves. A loud breeze rushed through the topmost branches but left me untouched. I knew the boulder-strewn wilderness well, and my woodlore had grown more skillful since my initiation into the band. While we had no serious adventures to occupy ourselves, there was still hunting to be done.

My anxiety tripled as I crested a final hill and started down into a rocky dell that sheltered the dragon's den, a broken shadow in the rock surrounded on all sides by shattered boulders and dead foliage. The lump in my throat felt larger than any dragon could ever be. The wind had disappeared, and even the birds were silent. A terrible stench wafted up, smelling faintly like something Reegas might have cooked.

I crept forward, drawing my sword, wondering why the ground was shaking and then I saw that it was only my knees. Panic flooded my senses—or had my senses left me? Me?

Against a dragon? A big scaly thing with bad breath and an awful prejudice against armed warriors?

The boulders offered some protection as I danced from one to another, moving closer to the dragon's lair. Fumes snaked out of the cave, stinging my eyes and clogging my throat, tempting me to choke and give away my presence. I could hear sounds of muffled breathing like the belching of a blacksmith's furnace.

I slid around a slime-slick rock to the threshold of the cave. I froze, an outcry trapped in my throat as I found the shattered ends of Alsaf's staff, splintered and tossed aside among torn shreds of black fabric. I swallowed and went on.

A few steps deeper into the den I tripped on the bloody remnants of Oldahn's studded leather jerkin. His bent and blackened sword lay discarded among bloody fragments of crunched bone.

On the very boundary of where sunlight dared to go, I found Reegas's rusty chainmail, chewed to a new luster and spat out.

A scream welled up as fast as my guts did, but terror can do amazing things for self-control. If I screamed, the dragon would know I had come, the latest in a series of tender victims.

But now, upon seeing with utmost certainty the fates of my comrades, my fellow warriors, anger and lust for vengeance poured forth, almost, *almost* overwhelming my terror. The end result was an angered persistence tempered with extreme caution.

Leg muscles tense to the point of snapping, I tiptoed into the cave where I stood silhouetted against the frightened wall of daylight. The suffocating darkness of the dragon's lair folded around me. I didn't think I would ever see the sun again.

The air was thick and damp, polluted with a sickening stench. Piles of yellowed skulls lay stacked against one wall like ivory trophies. I didn't see any of the expected mounds of gold and jewels from the dragon's hoard. Pickings must have been slim in the kingdom.

I went ahead until the patch of sunlight seemed beyond running distance. My jerkin felt clammy, sticking to my cold sweat. I found it hard to breathe. I had gone in too far. My sword felt like a heavy, ineffective toy in my hand.

I could sense the lurking presence of the dragon, watching me from the shadows. I could hear its breathing like the wind of an angry storm but could not pinpoint its location. I turned in slow circles, losing all orientation in the dimness. I thought I saw two lamp-like eyes, but the stench filled my nostrils, my throat. It gagged me, forcing me to gasp for air, but that only made me gulp down more of the smell. I sneezed.

And the dragon attacked!

Suddenly I found myself confronted with a battering-ram of fury, blackish green scales draped over a bloated mass of flesh lurching forward. Acidic saliva drooled off fangs like spears, spattering in sizzling pools on the floor.

I struck blindly at the eyes, the rending claws, the reptilian armor. The monster let out a hideous cry, seething forward, fat and sluggish to corner me against a lichen-covered wall. My stomach turned to ice, and I knew how Alsaf, Oldahn, and Reegas must have felt as they faced their death.

LET ME DIGRESS A MOMENT.

Dragons are not exactly best-fed of all creatures living in the wild. Despite their size and power, and the riches they hoard (but who can eat gold?), these creatures find very little to devour, especially in a relatively small kingdom like our own, where most people live protected within the city walls. Barely once a week does a typical dragon manage to steal a squalling baby from its crib or strike down an old crone gathering herbs in the woods. Rarer still does a dragon come across a flaxen-haired virgin (a favorite) wandering through the forest.

Hard times had come upon this particular dragon. Only impending starvation had driven it to increase its attacks on the peasantry, forcing the king to offer his daughter as a reward to rid the land of the beast. The future must have looked bleak for the dragon.

But then, unexpectedly, a feast beyond its wildest dreams! This dragon had greedily devoured three full-grown warriors in half as many days, swallowing whole the bodies of Alsaf, Oldahn, and Reegas.

And so, when the dragon lunged at me in the cave, it was so *bloated* and overstuffed that it could barely drag its bulk forward, like a snake which had gorged itself on a whole rabbit. Its bleary yellow eyes blinked sleepily, and it seemed to have lost heart in battling warriors. But it snarled forward out of old habit, barely able to stagger toward me.

I won't, by any stretch of the imagination, claim that killing the brute was easy. The scales were tougher than any chainmail I could imagine, and the dragon didn't particularly want its head cut off, but I was bent on avenging my friends and winning myself a princess. If I could just accomplish this one thing, I could call myself a warrior. I would never have to prove myself again.

Alsaf, Oldahn, and Reegas had already done much of the work for me, dealing vicious blows to the reptilian hide. But I still can't begin to express my exhaustion when the dragon's head finally rolled among the cracked bones in its lair. I slumped to the floor of the cave, panting, without the energy to drag myself back out to fresh air.

After I had rested a long time, I stood up stiffly and looked down at the dead monster, sighing. I had won myself a princess. I had avenged my comrades.

But perhaps the best reward was that I could now call myself a real warrior, a dragon-slayer. I imagined I could think of a few ways to make the story more impressive by the time I actually met my bride-to-be.

The monster's head was heavy, and it was a long walk to the castle.

Great." Ild waved Sir Kendell out of the room's middle. "Stupid story, you didn't do shit, not a hero, siddown and shut up."

"I did slay a dragon," Sir Kendell protested.

"So murdering a defenseless lizard makes you a hero?" A smirk crept across Ild's lupine features.

"It would have recovered." Sir Kendell drew himself erect. "I'm sure I saved somebody."

"Atli," Ild said, "when this is over, chop this guy's head off first."

The troll winked his assent at the imp. Though he took no particular joy in killing Ild's victims, he owed the little painted demon. When they met, the troll had been overwhelmed with grief and guilt from the deaths of his grandchildren. Ild took all that away. Allowed the huge warrior to function as a proper troll should.

He would do anything to repay that debt.

"Well, girl," Ild turned his beady little eyes to Masika, "your turn. No one has been equal to the task yet, and I am going to say it doesn't look good for your team. Give us your story."

Masika picked her way through the crowd and the shattered bits of table to the middle of the room. She smoothed the front of her long coat, looked around herself, and began.

THE WRONG WAY TO BUILD A SEX DUNGEON
KEVIN PETTWAY

The Fell Citadel reared up in front of the delegation, twisted spires clawing the blue sky in a murderous attempt to disembowel the few puffy white clouds overhead. Masika stared past the city of Dismon with its work crews and burned remains at the warped palace. The one painting of the citadel she had seen depicted a squat, ugly, utilitarian building of black stone that brooded down over Tyrrane's capital city. This thing looked like it had been turned to gigantic teeth and poisoned antlers.

It was *fantastic*.

"Papa. *Papa*." Masika grabbed at Tennat Oburn's arm and pointed to a section of the citadel's roof. It lay ruptured in the sun, an exposed belly torn open and frozen in time, walls ripped and pulled high. At this distance it was impossible to see what lay within.

The young woman, half a year past sixteen, did not turn to see if her father was looking. "That's where it happened. That's where the Hill Fury won. That's where she beat the Anger Under the Mountain and saved the Thirteen Kingdoms."

"Yes, my lahamila, I know." His smile, tired from the journey and—if Masika were being honest—far too much information about the Hill Fury, lit a warm fire in her heart. "I was there when the Holy Emperor related the tale. Standing at your side if I recall. Let us speak only in Andosh from here out. Darrish may be the more beautiful and sophisticated language, but we will be seen as condescending if we use it in the Fell Citadel."

"Yes, Papa."

Lahamila was his pet name for her. It referred to the brilliant and beautiful flares of purple and gold light that reflected off the Flame Cliffs at sunset. To Masika they meant boldness and daring.

To her father's opposite side, Meritities rolled beautiful eyes heavenward and pursed full lips. Masika's older sister did not approve of her enthusiasms and was determined to undermine the Hill Fury's memory any time she could. Still, beyond her elegant and silent display of frustration, she did not mock Masika.

This time.

Shouting workmen pulled Masika's attention as they winched a tall wooden frame upright, rebuilding Dismon one home at a time. They did not dress for the chill, their pale bodies long acclimated to the constant wintry conditions here. Masika, her father, and the entire Egren delegation, by contrast, were wrapped tight in as many layers as they could wear and continue to move. The bright colors of their clothes, in golds, reds, and greens, as well as their dark faces, marked them as alien as they could possibly be in this dour place.

The citizens watched them pass, though without the hostility Masika expected. Just three months ago these people had been at war with Egren, although none of that had been the doing of anyone out here. A cold breeze blew the stink of old fires and charred timber into her face.

They were here as an official proxy to Holy Emperor Khasek V of Egren, Masika's uncle and her father's eldest brother.

Tennat Oburn had a reputation for honesty and compassion—unlike the rest of the family—that made him the perfect representative for missions like this. He was to express sympathy without responsibility and see if he could tease out any new opportunities for trade that would benefit Egren. Meritities, a shark in Egren court circles, was here to watch their father's back and listen when no one else was.

Masika had no formal place in the proceedings, but there was no way she would let her father travel to the site of the Hill Fury's greatest victory—and her death—without her. Tennat Oburn doted on Masika, which contributed to Meritities disdain, and had allowed her to train with her granduncle (on her mother's side) Mahu, a member of the emperor's Veiled Breath. Tennat trusted both of his daughters far more than their mother felt was wise.

"Do you think the Hill Fury's body will be here? No, probably not. King Keane probably took it back to Greenshade with him."

Tennat chuckled and patted his daughter on the head while Meritities looked away. Behind them, the rest of the delegation trudged and shivered in front of their carriages. They were here to be seen offering support, whether or not they actually provided any.

"Can we go to Greenshade next?"

THE STATE FUNCTIONS TENNAT, Meritities, and the rest of the diplomats attended proved unutterably boring, and Masika soon vanished to search the citadel on her own. Her sharp-eyed mother would never have allowed it, but Papa took his job seriously and was easily distracted from watching inquisitive teenagers.

Not that he would have stopped his favorite daughter anyway.

After visiting the throne room above—the place torn open to the heavens where the Hill Fury destroyed the demigod Angrim, the Anger Under the Mountain—Masika decided to go low and see the catacombs where Angrim had lived for hundreds of years, maybe even longer. She borrowed a lamp from a servant and tarried a moment at the doorway to the deep corridors, a chill in both her flesh and her soul. The brightly colored linens she wore, patterned and flowing, were beautiful but not warm.

"Scary place, isn't it?"

Masika whirled, her hand on the hilt of her knife, to face a man in a wheeled chair, an expression of wry amusement on his face.

"You're a pretty little thing." The man was thin with a pointed beard, once dark red but now mostly gray, and he sported a jagged scar that ran down his forehead, beneath an eyepatch, and over one cheek. "Egren delegation? You must be Tennat Oburn's youngest. Mastika?"

Little? Who did he think ... Oh. Her hand dropped away from the knife.

"Masika, Your Grace." She bowed her head. The man was Prince Cantil Swiftheart, brother to Queen Jasmayre. She might be in a bit of trouble here. "I was just—"

"Getting away from the boring old shits upstairs and looking to see where the Anger did all his angering?" Cantil grinned at her, open and disarming.

"Yes, sir." Tension released from her taught limbs. Would she become the first to see the Anger's lair outside of Dismon's royal family? Pride swelled in her chest.

"Well, come along then, and we'll go check it out. I was the one who found the soul of the dragon's wife down there, you know. I saved Greenshade. At the very least."

Masika's head cocked to one side. "I thought the Hill Fury did that."

"Issta's Gates, girl," Cantil said, waving an arm in front of himself. "Isn't it enough that woman got credit for everything else, now you want to give her mine too?"

It took another twenty minutes to get down to the actual nest of the dead monster. Cantil was extraordinarily adept at navigating his chair, controlling it to the extent that even the numerous stairs offered little obstacle.

Acrid mold polluted the freezing air. Cantil held the lamp and illuminated Angrim's black stone chambers. Rotting shelves held broken bottles in the front room, and the adjoining chamber was another filled with human remains. A shattered mirror frame stood sentinel over a hallway floor covered in bright edges, and a green wooden door lay open into a tiny library of musty books.

The feeling of being in a haunted place of ancient evils that watched with malevolent hatred was easy enough to ignore. Masika, after all, had a *sister*.

Excitement vibrated her arms and legs. Meritities would die to know where Masika was this moment. Or maybe not. Meritities did not seem to care much for anything that could not be done in an expensive gown and a face full of makeup.

"This is where we found Dad," Cantil said, gazing at the cracked stone floor. "Jazz said Angrim kept him alive long enough to understand exactly what he was doing to his daughter. How he was breaking her body and turning her into his creature."

"That must have been awful for him." Masika did not have as many details of Queen Jasmayre in her "Jazmonster" form as she wished, but she knew enough to surmise that the process of creating her could not have been pleasant.

"I'm not happy it happened to Jazz," Cantil said, still staring into the past, "but as for Dad? Well, I'm sure it was no night in the whorehouse, but he probably deserved a lot worse."

"What's that?" The stone wall, while not smooth, held an obviously manmade alcove above their heads, no more than six inches square. Curiosity flared in Masika. Had no one ever seen this before? Was she about to make a new discovery?

"Just a shelf of some kind cut into the wall. It's empty."

Masika moved to the far side of the hallway and stood on her toes. The small space was too dark to see into. With a running start she jumped, billowing pants and coat whipping in the sudden movement, and caught hold of the edge with both hands. She pulled herself up until she could peer within.

"I guess I didn't look that close." Cantil rolled his chair next to Masika's dangling form. "Any fascinating cosmic artifacts? Maybe a magic serving fork?"

A strange seam ran almost invisibly around the back wall of the tiny alcove, creating a smaller panel. Masika reached in and pushed against it. The panel pressed a half-inch backward, and with a loud click, the wall Masika hung from swung into the hall several inches.

It was *thrilling*.

"That's new." The chair backed away from the wall, and Masika dropped to the ground.

She moved to the side of the stone door and pulled against it, her young muscles opening the portal against the grating hinge hidden inside the wall. After pulling it far enough to accommodate Cantil's chair, they both looked within the black and sickly sweet smelling chamber.

The walls were lined with workbenches and shelves supporting a variety of odd implements, most of which Masika could not fathom the use of. They all looked as if their application were intended to bring harm or pain somehow. But the instant she spied the two figures in the center of the room Masika forgot about the strange tools.

The pair of stone tables rose to Masika's shoulders, and the bodies atop them were covered in filthy sheets. The smell in the room snapped into place as that of old wounds allowed to fester. She stepped in and lifted one of the sheets, leaving it in place where it stuck to the body beneath.

What had the Anger left behind?

The naked corpse of a man stared at her; his pallid skin covered in faintly glowing blue tattoos. Scattered wounds oozed or crusted or adhered to the stained sheet.

"This isn't right." Masika pulled the sheet up around the edge to expose a thick chain, rusted and pitted, draped over the body. "He's been here no less than three months. Why does he smell like untended injuries instead of rot? He's gray, he's …" She touched the man's chest, careful to avoid the tattoos. "He's cold. What was the purpose of this?"

"It looks similar to what Angrim did to Jazz, just—I don't know—less refined?" Cantil scratched at his pointed little beard and sat up straight to see better. "Maybe this guy was practice."

Her father would be thrilled at what she had unearthed. New information about the Anger could only increase his standing here. Meritities would be irritated at the distraction, but who cared what *she* thought? And as for Masika, any discovery relating to Queen Jasmayre was but one step away from the Hill Fury herself.

The corpse's eyes turned to Masika.

"Allz's wounds! This man is alive." Masika moved around the table, frantically pulling at the cloth where she could and lifting the man's head. As Masika rounded the table to pull more of the chains, Cantil wheeled himself backward and bumped into the wall behind him with a squeak.

The man on the table followed Masika with his gaze but said nothing.

"I think maybe we shouldn't disturb anything down here yet." Cantil eyed the exit as he spoke. "Let's get Jazz in on this. Angrim had some dangerous—oh, you're already doing it."

Masika lifted the heavy chain from the man's chest, and a second one that draped over his thighs. He immediately fell to coughing and reached out to the second figure on the other table.

"You want me to get that one too?" Running around the foot of the man's table, Masika repeated her actions on what turned out to be a dirty and beaten woman of unearthly beauty, with similar tattoos cut into her skin.

Masika was going to be a hero.

"Oh, yes." Cantil craned his neck. "We should definitely free *her*. Could be important."

The instant Masika removed the second chain from the woman, pale like her counterpart but with a frail cast he lacked, she sat upright, shrieked, and with a sound like the whipping of crisp linens on a sunny day, vanished in a cloud of dust. In her place a loudly screaming bird flapped away into the furthest corner of the room and lit upon a high shelf.

"I was not expecting that." Masika turned back to the door, where Cantil continued to back away. "What's wrong?"

"'What's wrong'? Why aren't you running? Aren't you afraid?"

"Should I be?"

Cantil widened his eyes and waved an arm to encompass the coughing man and the squawking bird. "Yes?"

The man coughed up something gray and stringy, leaned toward the bird, and spoke to it in an unfamiliar language. He pushed himself off the end of the table and shuffled toward the excitable animal.

"I think he must be speaking bird." Masika gawked and grinned. Had she also discovered a new language? She couldn't wait to find out how this tied into the Hilly Fury's story.

"We definitely need to get Jazz," Cantil said.

"HE'S SPEAKING *Metzoferran*." Queen Jasmayre leaned forward to the man, still clad only in the soiled sheet. "It's the language of the gods. Of magic." Her eyes narrowed, and her mouth drew tight in her thin face. Her tight black clothes and pale white face set her red hair alight, as if she were a long, bony candle. Not attractive, exactly, but her intensity more than made up for it.

She was so *poised*. Every movement purposeful, every glance had meaning. Masika found herself unconsciously imitating the way the queen stood.

"Ask him if he's met the Hill Fury." Excited, Masika leaned forward, but frowned and stepped back against the wall at Meritities's irritated glance. Her taller, more beautiful, and much more *perfect* sister might be an incredible pain in Masika's side, but she knew her way around royalty. Masika would be a fool not to heed her warnings.

Queen Jasmayre spoke to the man in the same language. He looked intently at her, sighed, and responded.

"What does he say?" Tennat Oburn frowned in sympathy with the man's bereft expression. "He looks so sad."

"His name is Rainn," Queen Jasmayre answered. "He is of the Alir."

"This guy's a god?" Cantil shook his head. "Angrim had a sex dungeon down here for gods?"

"I don't believe it was for sex." Queen Jasmayre asked another question, to which Rainn merely shrugged. "I believe Angrim was perfecting the techniques he used on me."

"Toldja," Cantil said with a smirk to Masika.

"Can we get them food and clothing? They must be starved." Silken voiced, Meritities's comment nonetheless caught Queen Jasmayre off-guard, who seemed to have forgotten her presence. Cantil's gaze, however, lingered over Masika's older sister.

"What about the bird-goddess?" Masika watched as the bird nervously eyed the room from its high perch. Glittering emerald eyes and pointed black bill, soft gray feathers with a lighter gray face and swooping black crest, it had the look of a water bird, though with a shorter neck and stouter body.

"She is Heron." The queen crossed her arms and tapped the side of her chin. "These two have been here since the citadel was built, which happened when men still made war with sticks and rocks. According to Rainn, she has been trying to fly away for over a thousand years, and now that she finally can, she appears to be stuck."

"What do they want now?" More than anything else, Masika felt a sense of responsibility for these two growing in her chest. Gods though they might be, they were broken and fragile. What would the Hill Fury have done in this situation? She barely thought at all about how irate Meritities would be at all the adulation Masika would receive from the Tyrranean Royals for saving two of their gods.

"We must return home," said Rainn, his Andosh cut with a melancholy flavor. "We're dimin ... Our abilities are compro— we're screwed as long as we're here. In the Alireon we'll be restored." His head drooped. "I gotta feel the weather. The wind, rain. To scratch my own crotch again."

His words carried weights of sadness within them, but they only stiffened Masika's resolve. Except that last part.

"That sounds horrible, but you couldn't have spoken to us in Andoshi before we ran upstairs to get the queen?" Cantil caught Masika's look. "Before Masika ran upstairs?"

Masika had been the one to wake them, and she would need to see them taken care of. She could not bear the thought of handing them off to someone else now. Not when she had just gotten them. "Then I'll take you. It can't be too far, can it?" That's what the Hill Fury would have done. She looked at her father and at Cantil and ignored her sister. Her father shrugged to indicate his lack of knowledge.

"Fuck if I know," said Cantil.

"The pass that leads to the Alireon is three days from here." Rainn stopped speaking when Heron screeched, and a pained expression stole across his plain features. He closed his eyes. "Because *we* can't fly."

The bird screeched again.

"Not unless you're gonna go without me," he said to the feathered goddess.

Heron quieted and scanned the room.

"I cannot accompany you at present, lahamila. It would be disrespectful to our hosts." Tennat Oburn smiled his tired-eyed smile at Rainn. "I am certain you would not mind waiting a few more weeks."

"I'm not going." Meritities crossed her arms in a smooth gesture that spoke of elegance, control, and disdain in equal measure. "We have been tasked by the Holy Emperor to—"

"I didn't ask you," Masika interrupted.

Whatever response Rainn might have made to Tennat's suggestion to wait was drowned out by Heron's wild screeching and flapping about the upper corners of the room.

"Apparently we'd rather die than not go now," Rainn said, his face a portrait of sadness.

You'd feel even worse about it if you knew how boring the diplomatic stuff they're talking about is, Masika thought.

"Then the Host will provide you with your guard." Queen Jasmayre waved a hand to indicate the matter resolved. She raised a brow in Masika's direction. "*You* will have something more interesting to do than listen to trade negotiations and roaming unfamiliar palaces unattended." She cut her eyes to Prince Cantil. "And *we* will have uninterrupted space to resolve our discussions."

That would be terrible. Masika wanted to be the one to help

them. She did not want to share such a singular experience with a dozen foreign soldiers.

"I find this to be an entirely acceptable arrangement." Tennat smiled and nodded to Queen Jasmayre, the very picture of genteel civility. "I will have no qualms about my daughter's safety under the watch of the queen's most generously supplied guard." He finished with a pointed stare toward his youngest child.

Heron let out a low, jittery squawk. Rainn shook his head.

"No, Queen. We don't trust your men. They can't go."

"And precisely who do you trust here?" Queen Jasmayre asked. "Or do you intend to limp there without a guard and guide?"

Heron squawked, and Rainn pointed a dirty finger directly at Masika.

"We trust her."

MASIKA LEFT with Rainn and Heron on horseback, headed northwest out of Dismon. Queen Jasmayre provided them with a map of the mountains and the foothills leading to them, though no one knew where the mythical pass to the Alireon might lay.

It was hardly Masika's fault if the guards were expecting to leave the next day. She and the two gods preferred an early exit. Queen Jasmayre wasn't *her* mother, and her father would get over it as soon as he saw how successful Masika was doing things her own way.

The mid-morning day was bright and sunny, and once they left the confines of the charred city, the air smelled of grass, wildflowers, and cold mountain air. This was going to be perfect. A few days with the literal gods of the Andosh, her stuffy sister left behind in the dark citadel, then she would return to her father and head to Greenshade, the home of the Hill Fury. Her life could not be any more glorious.

Squawk!

"Heron sees the soldiers the queen assigned to us. Guess they didn't wait the whole day once everyone figured we were gone." Rainn put a gloved hand up to shield his eyes and looked skyward at Heron. "We gotta lose them or she's gonna fly off on her own. She'll probably get lost or killed." The god's sorrowful demeanor had not changed since his release from Angrim's dungeon. Even the vest the Tyrraneans dressed him in was dark and blue, like an evening thunderstorm.

At Rainn's long sigh, Masika glanced up. Why was he so sad? She would have been ecstatic to be freed from such horrific confinement after so long. Making him feel better would be another fine accomplishment in her ever-growing list of accolades.

He pointed his chin north at the first crusty outcroppings where the Bitter Heights foothills began their arduous climb. "That way. The mountains'll hide us from men."

They turned and increased their pace, and Heron flew down to light on Rainn's shoulder. They had one horse each for her and Rainn to ride, another for spare, and a fourth pack animal. The beasts had been chosen for docility and followed Rainn easily enough.

Once in the foothills, Rainn twisted through unseen ravines and narrow pathways until Masika had no idea where they were. The trails were certainly not on the queen's map. Just as abruptly, they left the rocky obscurement and entered a low, grassy meadow between the mountain's broad toes.

"That oughtta do it." Rainn said. "For all it matters."

"I may have no hope to understand," Masika said to him, "but why aren't you happy to be going home? You've been miserable ever since you woke up. You're not chained to a stone table any longer, the day is beautiful, and you'll soon be with family." Masika grinned at Rainn. "I'm so excited for you. Your life is already so much better than it was just yesterday, and it's only improving from here."

Rainn squinted and looked up into the wondrous blue sky. His mouth turned down so far Masika thought he may be about to cry. He pulled at the bottom of his thick woolen vest so that it better covered the gray, long-sleeved shirt underneath. "I've come back to sadness and pain. The world's a dry handjob with a fistful of sand."

He rode on.

By noon the brilliant sun provided enough warmth for Masika to remove the fur-lined cloak Queen Jasmayre had gifted her with, leaving her in a sleeveless yellow kaftan with red trim and wide yellow pants. They crawled up into the first long flat valley between foothills and encountered an encampment of refugees. From the black and gray floppy hats, ruined clothing, and scorched belongings, Masika judged them to be from Dismon. There had to be two hundred souls here.

Buzzing flies joined the smells of unwashed bodies and the stink of old fires, which Masika was beginning to think was following them everywhere. The refugees watched them with greedy eyes set in dirty faces.

"They're gonna kill us for our food." Rainn said this without alarm, as though being murdered were something that happened to him every day.

Perhaps it had been.

Less content to be killed, Heron launched herself into the air so fast she did not even screech her fear. The goddess climbed higher and higher, until she was no more than a wheeling speck against the crystal blue.

"Gonna be a meal for hawks," Rainn stated, gazing upward.

"Rainn, you should be ashamed." Masika made an effort to look stern, though Rainn did not turn in her direction to see it.

"You know how skittish Heron is. These people are no threat. They're afraid and hungry and—"

"Down off them horses. Now."

A man in his early sixties, thin and rangy with tied-back gray hair and wearing the well-worn armor of the Tyrranean Host stood in the path through the camp in front of them, a half-dozen ruffians spread out behind him with more filtering in from the sides. His voice was even and held no cruelty in it, but it carried the cadence of one well-used to being obeyed.

Rainn slid from his mount's back, unbuckled his borrowed sword belt, and dropped it between himself and the soldier. "There. That oughtta make it easier for you to kill us and fuck our corpses. Unless you'd rather torture us to death. I've been away for a while, so I'm not sure how people like to do that sorta thing anymore."

One brow raised above the soldier's flinty eye, and he glanced at Masika. "You too, goozy."

Without moving from her horse, Masika straightened her spine and glared down at the soldier. Goozy meant *gold* in Pavinn, and people everywhere used it as an epithet against the Darrish, whom they thought were all rich. It stung more because in her case, it happened to be true.

Masika hoped she looked intimidating to the soldier. "Before this goes any further, you ought to know that I am a warrior of the emperor's Veiled Breath. I am certain I am more than a match for any number of poorly armed brigands."

"Uh-huh." The soldier leaned down and picked up Rainn's sword. He drew it, inspected it, and swapped it with the one at his side, which he handed to the man next to him. That man took it and handed his pitchfork to the next in line. "What's a Veiled Breath? Never heard of it."

"That's because we are a highly secretive group of skilled fighters." A smile crept across Masika's face. Intimidating this rube would be simple for her. "We serve as the emperor's hidden right hand."

"Secret, huh?" A matching smirk appeared on the soldier. "Why're you tellin' *me* about it then?"

"Well, um …" She had not thought this entirely through. "I just want you to know what you're up against before you make any rash decisions."

The soldier grinned and waved to her to dismount. "Get down. No one's gonna hurt you. But we *are* takin' your food and weapons, and them horses. Havin' mounts'll make hunting for this lot easier. Even if you was a Breathy Whatsit, you're still gettin' dragged offa that horse."

With thirty or so desperate-looking men and women moving to surround her, Masika judged the old soldier was telling the truth. The Hill Fury would never have let herself get into a situation like this.

She hopped from the horse's back and stalked up to stand beside Rainn. "I think you could have been more supportive here."

"What's the point?" he asked.

"Hang on." Masika raised her hands to the oncoming crowd of filthy refugees. She needed to reassert control here. "I'll give you the provisions and two of the horses, but we need to keep the other two for riding and our weapons for hunting and defense. I don't want to hurt anyone."

The soldier rolled his eyes. "Fine. I'll fight you for it. I win, I get everything, you win, you leave with all your crap. That sound fair?"

"Good a way to get murdered as any," Rainn replied.

"He wasn't talking to you." Masika drew her desert blade and cut the air. "I accept your terms. May I know the name of the man I'm about to kill?"

At this the soldier actually laughed. "Sure. I'm Dider. Used to be a sergeant in the Host 'til Angrim burned us all down. Now I'm the leader of lost souls lookin' to make a new life somewhere far from the hell and misery." He drew the blade he'd just taken from Rainn and nodded. "And you? I need to know where to send the body and my apologies to your momma."

"Masika. And the rest won't be necessary." She whipped the sword up and pointed her blade at his face.

"Mother Love preserve you, for I shall not."

Seven seconds later Dider sat upright in the dirt, gingerly holding his empty sword hand and shaking his head.

Rainn sighed, picked up his sword and belt, and shuffled back to his mount.

"Can someone explain what burning fuckery just happened to me right there?" Dider asked.

"You just lost us our food and horses," someone grumbled from the crowd.

Masika sheathed her blade and held out her hand to help Dider to his feet. "Take all the horses and the food." She smiled and reached up to grasp his shoulder. It was hard as stone. "We can hunt for more to eat, and we're not in any real hurry. If it'll help you to provide for your people, it's worth the inconvenience."

If the extra animals and supplies would help cement Dider's leadership here and allow him to better lead these people out of danger, it was worthwhile for Masika to walk. Plus, a dramatic and sneakier corner of her mind whispered, it would make a much better story after she had led the two gods to safety if there were some additional hardships along the way.

She ignored the loud and long-suffering sigh from behind her as Rainn once more clambered down from his horse.

"You're a strange young woman, Masika. Hope the world never punishes you too harsh for it." Dider glanced around until he spied the dirty fellow he'd given his sword to, who dived into the crowd. "We're kinda hobbled out here right now, but if there's ever anything we, or I at any rate, can do to help, just find me. You done a good thing here today."

Good perhaps, but would it be enough to make a real difference?

"Dider," Masika lowered her voice, "we came from the citadel, and Queen Jasmayre sent some Host to follow us and ensure we were safe. We gave them the slip, but they may be following. If they encountered any deserters ..."

"Right." Dider craned his neck as if he might spot Host soldiers creeping up from beneath the rocks. "We'll be gone by the time they get here. I hope."

"Ask Mother Love's fortune," Masika said.

"Uh, sure. You too."

"Clear-Eyed Denari, how did I just do that?"

Masika stood in the midst of a cold and wide stream, her yellow pants rolled up past her knees, and gripped a struggling three-foot river eel in both hands. With a grunt she threw it to the side, where Rainn stared down at it and Heron jumped on it, stabbing it behind the head with her powerful bill.

That was amazing. She was like a gilded repent in the Yellow Sea, clawing fat and otherwise invisible beetles out of the desert sand.

"Heron's blessing." Rainn closed his eyes and reclined against the flat boulder behind him. "I told you that already."

"But I couldn't even see the eel." Masika peered into the slow-moving stream, reflections of sunlight and late afternoon sky making chaotic patterns in its surface. "Can I do it again?" Even Djephan, the more physical of her two older brothers, could never have done such a thing.

The stream appeared as a twisting blue brushstroke on the queen's map, though there was no name for it.

"As long as you're willing to stand in the freezing melt you can." Rainn did not open his eyes. "Your teeth're chattering, and your lips're blue, so I don't imagine you'll make it much longer 'fore you pass out and drown. Stay if you want, but we're not stopping to bury you."

Her hands really were shivering. Masika picked her way through the icy stream to the sand and rocks of the bank and felt as if she'd just stepped onto a warm desert dune. "How can she do that? Help me pluck an eel right out of the stream without even knowing it's there?"

With another sigh, Rainn lifted his head to answer. "Heron's the goddess of catching small animals in still or slow-moving water. If you'd tried up the mountain a ways where the stream's narrow and fast, you'd die of exposure before you turned up a fish."

"That's a very specific realm of divine power." Masika watched Heron, blue runes glowing through her feathers, lift the bleeding eel and bang it against a rock.

"Angrim took us because we're no threat to him, and because he figured the rest of the Alir wouldn't risk coming after us. Guess he was right about that." Rainn fell to watching Heron too, as she finished her casual murder and wiped her bill in the short grass. "He wanted easily controllable rats for his experiments."

"What are you the god of, Rainn?" Masika had been dying to ask ever since they left the Fell Citadel, but the question had not sounded polite in her ears. But since he had already brought it up ...

"You really the Emperor's Veiled Breath?" Rainn's eyes narrowed. "You seem a little fresh for an elite and secret imperial fighting squad."

"Oh, uh, no." Masika grinned, her nervousness at the sudden exposure bubbling up in an anxious giggle. "Well, almost. My uncle Mahu is, and he trained me to fight. Him and

Sabni. They're ... well, they're both in the Breath. Or they used to be."

Rainn pulled a blade of grass out of the bank and sat still, slowly tearing it into halves. "I'm the god of doing things out-of-doors in poor weather."

"Oh." Masika was not sure what the correct response was to that. There were one hundred and four members of the P'tak, the pantheon that watched over Egren and the other Darrish kingdoms. There were a few less important gods in there, but none so ... trivial? "That sounds like it could come in handy." She wanted to make him feel better. He was so glum about everything.

A vague frown clouding his features, Rainn stared up at the clear sky. "Maybe on a better day."

Of course. If he was the god of being useful in bad weather, he would have to feel pretty pointless when it was nice out. And the weather had been gorgeous for the last week. Poor Rainn.

If she could not help him, she would do something nice for Heron. Masika pulled her sharp dagger from her boot and moved to slice a strip off for the goddess. "You hungry?"

Heron erupted from the ground in an explosion of screeches and soft gray feathers, beating her terrified way into the air.

Standing rigid, lest she further traumatize Heron, Masika watched the squawking goddess as she rose into the air and raced over the crest of the next foothill. It was going to take a while before Masika got used to anyone being that scared of her.

"Maybe later, then."

THE QUEEN'S map got them into the right area, and Rainn led Masika to a hidden pathway sliced imperceptibly into the rock. Even watching him enter, she had to ask Rainn to stick out his hand so she could follow.

Only one of them could walk the smooth pathway at a time, so close were the high stone walls cut into the mountainside. The breeze whistled through and chilled Masika. Even Rainn buttoned his vest.

"Are you happy to be almost home?" Masika would have been, but she knew what Rainn was going to say before he answered.

"No." He plodded the narrow path as if it led to a gallows. "But the power's there. Familiar. I feel our home. Maybe if the family can lift whatever Angrim cursed us with, I might find less misery there."

Denari's eyes. Masika had forgotten. It wasn't the weather, or at least not just the weather. Rainn said Angrim had *screwed* them both. She wanted to know what that meant. See if there was any way she could help. But she supposed she was helping already. As much as she could. That had to count for something.

"Rainn?" Her father would have told her not to ask, but he wasn't here. "What did Angrim do to you? How did he, um, screw you?"

"He cut into us. Wrote runes into our bones." His voice was flat as he described their desecration. "Over and over, working out the best way to break us. By the time he was done, there was barely anything left. I'm hardly more than a man. Less, when the damn sun is out."

"Would you feel better if we had a little rain?"

"Maybe." He heaved a familiar sigh. "At my best, I was *everything* in a real mountain storm. Not even the other gods'd stand against me if the storms were grand enough. That's how strong I was. Except for Father Oldam himself, anyway." Rainn paused and twisted around to look at Masika. "I think some bit of that'd come back if the weather improved." He smiled a sad smile. "Maybe. It'd be nice to have a boner again."

"I think it'd be grand to teach you about modern conversational boundaries." Masika returned his forlorn expression with a sunny grin. "You'd make so many more friends."

But etiquette training, more Meritities bailiwick than Masika's, died on the vine. Instead, they climbed the rest of the day in silence. Heron watched her from Rainn's shoulder. Masika reached out to touch her smooth back and Heron hopped to Rainn's other shoulder. She neither screeched nor flew away though, so Masika considered it an improvement.

Halfway through the next day, the path widened to a dozen feet, and Masika's spirits flew. It was a signal that her act of kindness was almost finished and Heron and Rainn would soon be amongst their own and Masika would be on her way to Greenshade, where she would later meet her father and sister after they finished their deadly dull mission here in Tyrrane. How delighted would the Alir be to have their wayward children brought home?

The Hill Fury would have been every bit as proud of her as Meritities would be jealous.

The outer wall of the path was low enough for Masika to peek over now, and she gasped to see how far they had come in so short a time. This trail must have been enchanted with the magic of the gods.

Masika squealed just a little.

Abruptly, Rainn threw himself to the ground and Heron launched herself into the air with a mournful call, the sound of lonely wind and loss.

As she left the wall, Masika saw a huge boulder set in the center of the path. It was not so big as to block it entirely, though it would require a little squeezing to get around. She had been so engrossed with the view she might have walked right into it.

"Rainn! What's wrong?" Masika ran to the despondent god, who beat on the stone path with his fists. Tears rolled down his cheeks. Above them, Heron continued her song of fear and sadness.

"This is the end." He raised his head and Masika's feet stepped back of their own will rather than face that depth of anguish. "We'll *never* go home."

A pull she could not describe drew Masika to the boulder. Hunger? No, that was stupid. It was *attraction*. A hot flush went up her neck and into her face. Why was it any less foolish to be attracted to a huge rock than to be hungry for it?

The boulder was eight feet wide at the base and twice that tall. She reached out.

"Don't touch it!" Still prostrate on the stone pathway, Rainn's wide-eyed gaze flitted between the huge rock and Masika's hand. He shook. He was terrified. For her?

Ridiculous.

Warmth filled Masika's body when she pressed her hand against the stone. Warmth and ...

She hopped backward, embarrassed at her body's reaction. Rainn was suddenly at her side, pulling her away. He'd never seemed to show the slightest bit of interest in her well-being before this moment, yet now he was filled with worry.

"You all right?" Rainn lifted her arms and turned her in a circle. "Can you hear me? Can you answer?"

Somewhere close by, Masika heard Heron land.

"I'm fine." Masika pushed Rainn and his hands away. His touch, while respectful, was confusing to her in the moment. She stepped away from him and stared at the enormous boulder.

The longer she looked at it, the more human shaped it appeared. Those bulges to the sides could be elbows, and those up top were certainly the shoulders of a very muscular man. More and more details became apparent. He was kneeling on one knee, head forward, arms back and at the ready. A cloth stretched across his eyes over a weather-beaten face.

Randomly, Masika wondered if Prince Cantil back in the Fell

Citadel would be impressed to know that Masika had walked right up to High King Oldam, head of the Alir and chief among all gods of the north, and put her hand on his thigh. Probably not. Cantil had not seemed the pious sort.

"What's going on? Why is Father Oldam here, like this? Why won't he allow us to pass?" Rainn tore his gaze away from Oldam and looked into Masika's eyes. "And how aren't you dead?"

"I know why he's here." Masika searched through her memories of the mad northern gods and their bitter battles and rivalries, though she had no recollection of ever having learned any of it. Her eldest brother Kohmose knew all this stuff, but she barely ever listened to him.

Somehow, Masika knew these memories had been placed there by her touch. "Oldam pulled out his eyes and threw them into the sky to keep watch over the north. Then he set himself on this path and turned his body to stone to protect the Alireon. I don't know from who, and I don't know why he won't let you by." She canted her head right to look at the narrow passage to the side of the god. Without trying, she knew they would not be able to go through, even if they were not killed outright.

There was more, but Masika was uncertain how much she should say. Oldam was afraid of someone without a face. Someone of terrible power and purpose. But that hardly applied to the three of them.

"We should leave." Masika took Rainn's hand and led them back the way they'd come.

After a tense few hours descending the mountain trail, Masika stopped. Rainn's despondency was palpable, and Heron, riding his shoulder, hung her gray head.

They camped partway down the slope, in silence as bitter as the cold. This was supposed to have been finished, and Masika pointed toward Greenshade. Or more likely waiting another fortnight for her father and sister in Dismon, but *then* Greenshade. She would learn so much about the Hill Fury there. Instead, she was not certain what she should do. Her responsibility was over, but Rainn and Heron had given up. She did not want to leave them this way, but how long was she supposed to put her life on hold here?

A fitful sleep followed, tangled by cold and stone and whistling mountain winds.

Trilling coos from Heron woke her, and in the dim morning light Masika saw the goddess perched on Rainn's knee, conversing with him in stuttering bird sounds.

Masika rubbed her eyes and pushed herself into a sitting position. "Soul's glory." At Rainn's blank stare, she elaborated. "It's a Darrish good morning. What are you two talking about?"

"Heron's had a dream she feels is terribly important. A gray crane with a scar over its eye had a message for you." Heron pecked at Rainn to continue. He frowned and pushed her off his knee. "It said you oughtta keep being our guide in this world, and if you did, you'd find everything you were looking for."

"Oh." Masika crossed her arms over her knees. Leaving these two was going to be even more difficult than she had anticipated. They were so helpless and dependent on her. "Well, you know what they say about dreams."

A loud squawk elicited a wince from Rainn and Heron pecked at his boot. "Ow. Fine. I was going to say; I just forgot."

"What?" Masika asked, eager to get this over with.

"Heron says the crane wanted me to tell you its name was Sarah."

A jolt ran through Masika's spine, and she jumped to her feet. Sweat broke out in her palms, and she could not suppress a wild giggle.

Sarah was the Hill Fury's true name.

"You're not home, but there's no reason for us to stop trying to get you there." Masika put her hands on her hips and pulled for an authoritative tone. Her father told her that people would follow her as the flowers followed the sun.

He might have been a bit biased, but she hoped not.

"Just as I promised to bring you this far, I vow to you here that I will discover why King Oldam has refused you entry to the Alireon and that we will rectify it." That sounded good. She was convincing herself if no one else. "More than anyone, you both deserve to go home. That is, if you're willing to do it."

Please say yes. Please say yes. It's the Hill Fury ...

Heron gazed at Rainn and made a purring sort of noise. He rolled his bloodshot eyes and let out the longest sigh Masika had yet heard.

"There's another power, pretty far south of us." Rainn stared past the wall and out over the countryside far below. "It'll probably murder us, but if it doesn't, maybe it can help."

With a squawk and with a loud flap, Heron hopped from Rainn's shoulder to Masika's. She pushed her way into Masika's fur-lined hood and settled there.

Masika smiled and resumed the trek down the mountain.

It was an excellent start.

A tli stood silent, unwilling to breathe, lest he break the moment.

Had they finally found the right people to bring Ild's creator back from the Undergates? The girl showed resourcefulness and determination, but many here tonight had demonstrated those qualities. But she touched the body of High King Oldam himself and lived. That should not have been possible.

And her companions. Actual Alir?

Ild's frown displayed little, except he had not immediately ordered everyone to smile and await Atli's axe, generally the imp's favorite part of the evening.

"Ild?" Atli whispered. "Vat do yoo think?"

"You know if this goes wrong we'll have overplayed our hand." Ild's response told Atli he had already made up his mind.

"These people can go?" Masika took a step toward Ild, but Atli did not move to intervene. He knew it would not be necessary.

They had their heroes.

"Yeah, yeah. They can go." Ild snapped a clawed finger and the people in the room roused as if waking from a long sleep. A few vanished in softly popping blue glows. His attention returned to Masika.

"But you and I need to have a talk."

ACKNOWLEDGMENTS

Thank you to our Kickstarter supporters who helped bring this project to life: Gerg, Becca Lee Gardner, Zaepho, Shayna, Dave Ham, Leslie Bridgwater, Jan Montgomery, Ethan A. Cooper, Peter Sartucci, N.V. Haskell, D.Y. Freeman (Ynes), Jodie SH Cerra, jharris140@gmail.com, B. Daniel Blatt, Anita Buckowing, SubjectToGnome, Amy Bigelow, Kimball Gontz, Bryan H. Emick, Jennifer Schomburg Kanke, Carolyn Klucha, Jon Coleman, Angela Tucker, Vic Pawlowicz, Jock and Jennifer Hardesty, Jess Pagac, Susan Wilkerson, Andie Pennell, Roger Johnson, Alexandra, Reni Valentine, Manservant Heckubis, Nancy D. Greene, Pamala Johnson, and Vicky Zook.

And a special thank you to Jody Lynn Nye, Kevin J. Anderson, and Todd Fahnestock for helping us make the anthology special by adding stories from their unique universes.

Finally, we need to recognize Cricket for creating the dynamic cover art, Lena for producing the high-quality trading cards and the cover, Sara for making sure we didn't mess up our grammar or punctuation egregiously, and Kevin for creating those incredible interstitial bits to tie the stories together.

AUTHOR BIOS

Our Core *Misplaced Adventures* Authors

C.M. McGuire may or may not be a cryptid living in central Texas, spoken of only in hushed whispers in small circles. It is said she holds degrees in history and creative writing and, when away from her word processor, teaches. This can only be corroborated by her elderly dog and 2 cats, but thus far they are tight-lipped.

Ethan A. Cooper was born and raised in southern California, cutting his teeth on a steady diet of Transformers and Robotech, superhero comic books, sci-fi/horror movies, and scary radio dramas like The War of the Worlds and X Minus One.

These interests progressed, leading him to create comic books on 6x9 lined steno pads with friends, write serial fantasy on pre-Internet bulletin board systems, and collaborate on short horror stories with his brother. Eventually, he wanted to tell longer tales. His first novel, What Happened On My Space Vacation, is a sci-fi adventure for the teenager inside all of us. Other published works include the clown horror compilation

Phildlestix/Phidlestixx/Phidlestixxx, the children's fantasy story Songquest, and Angel Descending, the first of the epic sci-fi Downfall series,

While he plots perilous situations for his characters to endure and creates digital art, he enjoys living in East Texas with his wife and their three children.

William LJ Galaini has failed at more things than most folks even attempt. Given his refined process of failure, he has streamlined his wordcraft and now produces books, short stories, and game narratives that are about what he knows best; idealistic losers that save the day.

Jessica Raney grew up in the hills of southeastern Ohio looking for the Mothman and every other thing that goes bump in the dark Appalachian night. These days she resides in Houston, Texas and translates her love of Appalachia and dark things into stories that combine crime, fantasy, and horror into Appalachian Supernatural Noir. Her genre-blending series, *Tooth and Nail* showcases her love of all things creepy and quirky. When not writing, she's navigating Houston traffic and enjoying the Gulf Coast with a weird little dog named Gimli.

Follow her on Facebook, Twitter, and Instagram.

Jen Bair is an Air Force brat, Army veteran, and military wife. She and her husband shamelessly drag their four kids all over the world on one adventure after another.

She has jumped out of perfectly good airplanes, been on a flying trapeze, bottle fed a live tiger, and been a S.C.U.B.A. instructor. She's lived in the Philippines, Guam, Korea, and Germany and she fully believes in world exploration as a lifestyle.

She homeschools with her energetic Malinois in tow when

she's not planning the next family vacation. She loves traveling to foreign places, real or imaginary.

Her family is her life. Her writing is her passion.

Kevin Pettway hails from Jacksonville Florida and is the author of the Misplaced Mercenaries books, a funny adult fantasy series that was awarded by the NYC Big Book Club, a finalist in the 2022 Imadjinn Awards, and has received several professional write-ups in Kirkus Magazine for which the author did not even have to pay. He has published a modest number of short stories, both within and without the Mercenaries world, with more on the way. Most excitingly, Kevin's publisher, Cursed Dragon Ship Publishing, has threatened encouraged him to open his world to other authors, creating the Misplaced Adventures Shared Universe. There are currently six authors toiling away to bring even more humor, fun, and backstabbing murder into the world, with plans to add even more in the next few years.

Although the old stereotype about writers just wanting to be locked away in a darkened room with a typewriter is as true of Kevin as it is anyone else, the other thing he enjoys tremendously is going to conventions and meeting new people. (In writing, two opposing motivations in the same person are often used to create tension and conflict and engage reader interest. Now that you know his conflicting motivations you understand just how deep and fascinating Kevin is!)

He regularly attends a large number of popular culture conventions, selling books and telling stories to people who haven't heard them before while his wife Lena tries to ignore him. Feel free to walk up and say hi. Nothing makes him happier. (You might also express condolences to Lena, who has heard all the stories.)

River and Book, Kevin and Lena's two dogs, also love meeting people, but hotels rarely love meeting dogs, so they stay behind at the puppy resort. Canine fan-mail will be accepted and forwarded to the appropriate addressee.

Kevin thinks Strange New Worlds is the best Trek series, nudging The Orville off that top spot, and is enjoying the Tolkeinesque comedy The Rings of Power more than he thought he would. His favorite new author is Tamsyn Muir, and his favorite old author is Roger Zelazny. (He may be dead, but he's still selling!) He is also developing an obsession for kayaking, having discovered it late in life and is unable to get enough.

Despite being from Florida, Kevin still has all his own teeth and has never had a restraining order placed against him.

Our Guest Authors

Todd Fahnestock is an award-winning, #1 bestselling author of fantasy for all ages and winner of the New York Public Library's Books for the Teen Age Award. *Threadweavers* and *The Whisper Prince Trilogy* are two of his bestselling epic fantasy series. He is a winner of the 2022 Colorado Authors League Award for Writing Excellence and two-time finalist for the Colorado Book Award for *Tower of the Four: The Champions Academy* (2021) and *Khyven the Unkillable* (2022).

His passions are fantasy and his quirky, fun-loving family. When he's not writing, he teaches Taekwondo, swaps middle grade humor with his son, plays Ticket to Ride with his wife, plots creative stories with his daughter, and wrestles with Galahad the Weimaraner. Visit Todd at toddfahnestock.com.

Jody Lynn Nye has published over 50 books and more than 170 short stories. Among the novels Jody has written are her epic fantasy series, *The Dreamland*, beginning with *Waking In Dreamland* and five contemporary humorous fantasies. She wrote eight books with the late Robert Lynn Asprin. Her newest series is the

Lord Thomas Kinago books, beginning with *View From the Imperium* (Baen Books), a humorous military space opera novel.

Her newest books are *Moon Tracks* (Baen), a young adult hard science fiction novel, the second in collaboration with Dr. Travis S. Taylor. *Rhythm of the Imperium*, third in the Lord Thomas Kinago series; *Pros and Cons* (WordFire Press), a nonfiction book about conventions in collaboration with Bill Fawcett; and the 20th novel in the Myth-Adventures series, *Myth-Fits*.

Over the last thirty or so years, Jody has taught in numerous writing workshops and participated on hundreds of panels covering the subjects of writing and being published at science-fiction conventions. She also runs the two-day writers' workshop at DragonCon. In 2016, Jody joined the judging staff of the Writers of the Future contest, the world's largest science fiction and fantasy writing contest for new authors. She is now its Coordinating Judge.

Once a lifelong Chicagoan (though still a Cubs fan), Jody now lives near Atlanta with her husband Bill Fawcett, a writer, game designer, military historian and book packager, and three feline overlords, Athena, Minx, and Marmalade. Check out her website at www.jodynye.com. She is on Facebook as Jody Lynn Nye and Twitter @JodyLynnNye.

Kevin J. Anderson has published more than 175 books, 58 of which have been national or international bestsellers. He has written numerous novels in the Star Wars, X-Files, and Dune universes, as well as a unique steampunk fantasy trilogy beginning with Clockwork Angels, written with legendary rock drummer Neil Peart. His original works include the Saga of Seven Suns series, the Wake the Dragon and Terra Incognita fantasy trilogies, the Saga of Shadows trilogy, and his humorous horror series featuring Dan Shamble, Zombie P.I. He has edited numerous anthologies, written comics and games, and the lyrics to two rock CDs. Anderson is the director of the graduate program in Publishing at Western Colorado University. Anderson and his wife Rebecca Moesta are the publishers of WordFire Press. His most recent novels are *Clockwork Destiny, Gods and Dragons, Dune: The Lady of Caladan (with Brian Herbert),* and *Slushpile Memories: How NOT to Get Rejected.*

JOIN THE CURSED DRAGON SHIP NEWSLETTER

Love what you just read? Want more just like it? Sign up for our newsletter so you don't miss out on the adventure. You'll get:

- A free book for signing up
- Advanced notice of new releases
- First word of books on sale
- Opportunities for free books
- Most up-to-date information on author appearances.

We're busy and know you are too. We won't send more than one newsletter a month.

Register below.

Made in the USA
Columbia, SC
13 October 2024